PROMETHEUS' DAUGHTER

MATTHEW KARABACHE

ISBN 13: 978-0-9924470-1-4 (Paperback edition)
ISBN 13: 978-0-9924470-0-7 (Kindle edition)
ISBN 13: 978-0-9924470-2-1 (PDF edition)

www.matthewkarabache.com

www.facebook.com/matthew.karabache

Did I request thee, Maker, from my clay
To mould me Man, did I solicit thee
From darkness to promote me?

-- Paradise Lost, Book X, 743–745

I grew up in the ruins of Geneva. We lived in the old Sécheron subway station at the northern end of the central business district. If you could find a well-sheltered vantage point, during the day you could see what was left of the lake—a shimmering heat haze, just barely visible on the horizon.

The subway used to be an open-air train line. They dug out tunnels to replace them as the city grew. The tunnels sheltered us from the sun and made Sécheron a safe place for us to live. Sometimes I wonder what our childhood would have been like if the subway had never been built. Whether we would have survived at all—and, if we did, whether we would have grown into the same people.

The station housed just under a hundred people, including our family, and was just one of a handful of settlements that called the remains of the city 'home'. Our leader was a man named Renard Mercer, a resourceful older man who had lived in Paris before the world ended. Sécheron had an array of scavenged solar panels that collected enough electricity to keep us going day-to-day, so we were able to amass a respectable stockpile of fuel for the generators. Beneath the lowest level, the station had a water bore plunging deep into the earth, so we even had a reliable source of potable water. Two of the platforms were given over to hydroponics, giving us enough food for everyone to eat—most of the time, at least.

My brother and I were lucky to grow up in such a place. We had food, water, power…when I was young it felt like Geneva was the whole world. I didn't realise how well we lived compared to most others until I was much older.

My mother and Mercer were involved, though she never called him our father. I have vague memories of another man before that, but she never spoke of him to me. My grandmother lived with us back then as well. She was alive when the world ended; she had been only eight years old. She used to tell me about the world as it was before. 'It was so beautiful, Adele,' she would say. 'I wish you could have seen it.' She was thirty-nine when she died. I was eleven.

The subway tunnels could be dangerous, but they allowed people from the scattered communities to roam relatively freely through what was left of the central districts of Geneva, even during the day. When I was a child, my brother Travis and I used to sneak out to play in them, much to our mother's distress. We were young and did not yet comprehend the world we lived in and how precious we, as children, were.

We were never alone, of course. There were other children. Madeleine Devereaux and I were like sisters—we were around the same age and remained close friends for many years. Davin was slightly older, a mischievous little boy with an impish grin and quick fingers. There was another boy, Thierry, who used to play with us as well. I have only vague memories of him. One day after sneaking out, he didn't come home. We never found out what happened to him. Or at least, our parents never told us. We stopped playing in the tunnels after that.

My mother, Josette, styled herself a doctor and a chemist. She had found books on medicine and the physical sciences and taught herself. Sécheron was large enough and fortunate enough to be able to support a specialist like her, and she was well-liked and respected. She mixed the nutrient solution that the food grew in, rendering down and recycling the bodies of those who died to help feed those that were left. When the others inevitably injured themselves or took ill, she would treat the sick, clean and dress their wounds, set their broken bones, and do what little could be done for those unfortunate enough to be burned by the sun. Once I was old enough, she began to teach me as well.

When I was fourteen, she took ill. I did everything I could to save her, but it wasn't enough. I stayed up each day while the others slept, studying her medical encyclopaedias and textbooks. I was convinced that there was some secret that would let me save her, if I could only find it. It was hard, when she died. I swallowed my grief and did what was necessary—her body was rendered down and consigned to the nutrient solution that fed the crops that fed us. Sécheron mourned her passing, but the world continued on in her absence. People did not stop hurting themselves or falling ill, and so I took her place.

When I wasn't treating patients, I studied my mother's books, reading them over and over again. Once I'd learned all I could from them, I managed to scrounge up a few more mostly-intact volumes in the hospitals near the southern end of the city. The buildings there were once part of a university; a place of learning. Can you imagine it? Hundreds—maybe even *thousands*—of people all learning to be doctors and nurses and surgeons. When your entire world consists of less than a hundred people, the existence of such a place seems to verge on the absurd.

It was there, at that absurd, impossible place, that we found it.

I had organised for a group of scavengers to take another expedition to the hospitals. Have you done much scavenging? It can be quite surprising, really, how much useful material is still waiting to be recovered in some places.

3

After a few decades of survivors picking through the ruins you might imagine there would be barely anything left at all but in my experience, that is rarely the case. There are just so few people left, compared to before the end of the world, and most are limited to taking what they can carry easily. I myself had been to the hospitals three times before, yet we'd still always manage to return with enough to have made the trip worthwhile.

Maddy came along, as she always did. I was always able to depend on her. Accompanying us was Davin and his mentor—a slightly older man who went by the name of Gage. Gage was a mechanic, and many felt that he was personally responsible for much of the success of Sécheron. He had been the one to recover and install the solar panels that supplied our electricity, many years ago. Davin was learning his trade as I had learned mine from my mother. Gage had been on several expeditions to the hospitals before, and was more knowledgeable of their layout than anyone. I remember that Travis had wanted to come as well, but I made him stay behind. While he didn't have quite the breadth of knowledge and experience that I did, it was a constant worry that someone might seriously hurt themselves while I was away. Travis, at the very least, knew enough to provide emergency care until our return.

We followed the subway tunnels as they made their way south, passing beneath the decaying buildings of the city, and emerged at Genève. Just to the west of Genève station is a small settlement at Les Charmilles, a handful of families living together in the lower floors of an old department store partially buried in rubble. We had to pass by Les Charmilles before crossing the dry riverbed to get to the hospitals.

It was always a nerve-wracking experience to encounter a group of people outside of Sécheron, even when you recognised them as some of your closest neighbours. Despite generally friendly relations and frequent trade, altercations over scavenging rights were distressingly common. Worse, there were those who would steal or even kill if they thought they would not be caught. We never left the station unarmed. I had a small calibre service pistol that belonged to my mother before me, but I had been lucky enough to never have a reason to use it.

The university hospitals were a sprawling set of buildings that covered what seemed to be an entire city block, scarred and pitted by exposure to the sun. Scavenging in buildings was generally dangerous work. The risk of a sudden collapse or a chance meeting with a group of strangers constantly hung over one's head.

On this particular expedition, while exploring one of the low-set buildings around the easternmost side of the hospital grounds, I happened across a disused elevator shaft plunging deep into the earth.

'Useless, ignore it,' Gage said when I brought my discovery to the others' attention.

'It looks intact. What's down there?'

'We checked it out ages ago, back when your mum was still around. It's all sealed up. There's a set of big steel doors once you get to the bottom of the shaft, but we couldn't get 'em open.'

'Any idea what's down there?' I said.

Gage scratched at his bald scalp, shaking his head, 'No idea. Can't see in, and it's not on any of the maps we found. The doors are locked with one of those hand scanning things. No electricity here even if we had someone who could open them, anyway.'

'Could we take another look?' I persisted. 'There could be something of use down there.' I didn't quite know what had triggered it, but something about the elevator shaft or Gage's description of what lay below had sparked off an intense sense of curiosity. The feeling itched at the back of my brain, begging to be scratched.

Davin interjected, 'It couldn't do any harm to check it out, right?'

Gage looked doubtful, but offered no further resistance when Davin and I dropped our backpacks and began preparing for the descent. Secured by nylon ropes, the two of us were lowered down the shaft while Madeleine and Gage remained above. It was dark below and we weren't sure of its exact depth, so we cracked a glow stick and dropped it down first. The sickly green light of the chemicals probed feebly at the pitted concrete and rusted steel, the dim light heightening the sense of claustrophobia and anxiety that one feels when exploring such places.

The thought occurred to me that the ropes we had brought may not be long enough. However, after descending for several long minutes we reached the elevator at the bottom of the shaft. We touched down, ensuring that our footing was secure before we detached the ropes. The hatch on the top of the elevator was open and we climbed down into it before emerging into the short corridor beyond. The darkness here, beneath hundreds of tonnes of earth, was absolute, broken only by the frail illumination of our wind-up flashlights.

Immediately ahead of us, perhaps fifteen feet from the elevator shaft, lay a set of steel double-doors. Our lights crept over the metal, revealing a pair of small windows set into the doors at head-height and the black, dead screen of the biometric scanner that would have once allowed ingress to whatever lay beyond.

'Doors like this usually have a manual release,' Davin said, kneeling down next to the scanner. He dropped his flashlight down next to him and started to probe at the seams between the device and the wall, seeing if there was a gap he could use to pry the cover away.

'What do you suppose is in there?'

'No idea,' he said. 'Treasure?'

I grinned in the darkness. 'Probably.'

While Davin busied himself trying to access the door locking mechanism, I stepped close and tried to peer into one of the windows. It was pitch black inside. The way the toughened glass reflected the light of my flashlight made it difficult to see anything at all. I tried pressing my cheek right up against the glass and cupping my hand over my eye, touching the torch to the window just below my face. In this manner, I caught a glimpse of what looked like large work tables covered in bulky shapes.

'No use,' Davin said. He had managed to pry off the scanner cover and was shining his flashlight at the wiring behind it. 'I can't see anything that looks like a release.'

I touched the wall to the side of the door. Solid concrete; nothing short of a jackhammer or some kind of explosive would get us through by force. I grunted, frustrated, then turned on my heel and stalked back over to the elevator shaft. There, I scooped up a loose chunk of concrete about the size of a cricket ball and returned to where Davin stood by the doors. Hefting the concrete in one hand, I let out a yell as I smacked it as hard as I could against the glass. My war cry became a yelp of pain as it bounced off without so much as leaving a scratch. I dropped it and shook my hand. 'Ouch.'

'That probably won't work. Maybe if I got a crowbar and whacked at it for a good five minutes,' Davin said, trying not to smile. 'But it would be useless anyway. Those windows are way too small to get through.'

I made a disappointed sound in the back of my throat.

'Gage has an oxy-acetylene torch, back at his workshop,' Davin suggested, once we had exhausted all of our immediate options. 'The door isn't that thick. If we're careful, we could cut our way in.'

I felt my face flush in excitement. Davin smiled at me, down there in the dark, as our flashlights began to fade. That was when I kissed him properly for the first time. His lips were cracked and dry, but warm. He almost fell over in surprise.

We had grown up together, of course, and flirted and played silly kissing games as children do when they are young, but in the two years since my mother's death I had withdrawn into my own world of medical textbooks and science. Madeleine and I had been encouraged by our parents to explore our sexuality from an early age. With so many women sterile from radiation and so few children being born, for our species to survive it was necessary to discover whether a girl has the potential as early as possible. My grandmother was lucky, one of the few alive at the time not immediately rendered sterile, but she did not have another child after giving birth to my mother when she was fifteen. My mother had my brother and I almost six years apart. It was unlikely that she would have ever had a third child should she have survived.

When I stopped showing any sort of interest in sex, I could tell that it did not sit easily with the rest of the community even though no one spoke to me openly about it. I got the feeling that Mercer may have had words with some of the others behind closed doors. If anyone had brought it up, however, I would have told them that I already knew I was infertile. Not long after my mother's passing, I had spent some time studying ovulation and the reproductive cycle. Without access to any of the equipment I would need to administer a test I had no definite proof either way, but my irregular, thin menstruations and several other signs were all I needed to decide that it was true.

I knew that Davin and Maddy had been experimenting sexually for some time now, while I spent my time stitching wounds and reading about chemistry. However, Davin frustrated Madeleine and they had fought too many times for any sort of serious relationship to develop. I had thought about it before, of course, but up until that moment I had forced myself to ignore my hormones. Ostensibly, this was to focus on learning and fulfilling my role in the community. I see now that it was also partially due to some obstinate subconscious teenage rebellion, revelling in the restrained disapproval of the adults that I now saw as my equals.

When I kissed Davin there that night, however, it was like a dam had broken within me. Animal desire rose within me and I pressed up against him, raking my fingers down the taut muscles of his chest and stomach. His body responded immediately and I could feel him growing hard against me as we ground up against each other.

Once we returned to Sécheron, we snuck away to a secluded spot and spent much of the day making love while

9

everyone else slept. He had grown into a handsome young man, my Davin, full of insatiable teenage vigour. From that day on we spent whatever time we could spare exploring each other's bodies. It became something of an open secret—everyone knew what Davin and I were doing whenever we made our excuses and snuck off. Even so, just as before, no one ever brought it up.

- - -

The next few nights passed at an agonising crawl. I was anxious to return to the hospitals to investigate the sealed level, but I had responsibilities that ate up most of my time. The acidity of the nutrient solution that fed our crops had increased and needed to be balanced lest our food source die. Chemicals and medicines brought back by scavengers needed to be catalogued and sorted. Beyond that, there were always plenty of injuries requiring treatment.

Gage was the biggest hurdle. 'Canisters for this girl are scarce,' he said to me when I went to see him about borrowing the oxy torch. 'You use up some of what little we got, maybe later we don't have it when we need it.'

When Davin saw just how eager I was to explore the sealed rooms, however, he joined his voice to mine. 'It'll be worth it,' he said, his voice brimming with certainty. 'Something locked up tight like that, completely untouched? There's got to be chemicals and medicine down there.'

'It'll be worth it,' I repeated, willing it to be true.

Gage scratched at his head and sighed. 'I don't like the idea of risking my equipment like that, but go ask Mercer. I'll abide by what he says.'

Satisfied at making at least a little progress, I went to see Mercer. He was more receptive than Gage. With a little help I was able to convince him that—while it *was* a gamble—there was also a very good chance of it being, in his words, 'a worthwhile expenditure of the community's resources'.

'What do you mean, I can't come?' Travis had pestered me as I made preparation to head out. Once Mercer had given us the go-ahead for the expedition, my young brother had immediately volunteered to help out.

'You need to be here in case anything happens,' I told him. 'If an accident happens while I'm away, you're the next best doctor that Sécheron has. Mercer made the decision that you need to stay behind and I agree with him.'

'Fine…that makes sense, I guess.' There was a distinct note of disappointment in his voice. His enthusiasm for my discovery encouraged me nonetheless. Finally, we were able to take our leave and return to the hospitals.

We took the oxy-torch along with extra ropes and climbing equipment, and set out through the tunnels. A few hours later, we were at the bottom of the elevator shaft. Gage set about cutting through the bolts that locked the doors in place. The rest of us stood well back and waited while he worked. I paced, full of nervous energy that kept me in constant motion. When he had finished, Davin and I used a crowbar to pry the doors apart.

Once the gap was large enough to admit a person, I took a deep breath and cautiously stepped inside, sweeping my flashlight over the interior of the room. I was greeted by the sight of tables covered in darkened computer monitors and high-end scientific apparatus. Behind me, the others came through one at a time as I slowly advanced, taking in my surroundings. It was a medical laboratory of some kind; that much was obvious from a cursory inspection.

I'm not sure what I was expecting to find, but at first I was almost disappointed. While the equipment was advanced and looked mostly, if not completely, intact, most of it would be impossible to get up the elevator shaft. Even if we did manage to take it back to Sécheron, we simply didn't have the electricity to run it all. I realised I was still holding my breath and exhaled slowly before breathing in the smell of the place. The air was dry and scratched my throat on its way down into my lungs, hints of sterility and iodine reaching my nose.

There were doors leading off from the main room and we set about exploring the place. One area was flanked by rows of plexiglass enclosures. I walked down the centre aisleway, sweeping my light back and forth as my footsteps echoed hollowly on the tiled floor. Mummified corpses of mostly-recognisable animals lay individually segregated in many of the enclosures. Dogs, monkeys, the occasional sheep or goat.

There was a pair of cells set apart from the rest at the far end of the room. When I approached them, at first I took their contents to be the bodies of another pair of monkeys. As I drew closer and my flashlight illuminated the enclosures, however, I could see that they also contained small beds, faded blue tables and chairs, scattered scraps of yellowed paper and scrunched up bundles of filthy cloth. I knelt down next to the plexiglass, horrified once I realised what I was seeing, yet also entranced by the macabre sight. The remains were curled up in the foetal position, pressed up against the barrier that separated the two cells as though huddled for warmth or companionship. Even in their decayed state they were eminently recognisable for what they were…a pair of small children.

We explored further, passing through several more small separate labs before finding a small room containing a computer server rack and a large generator. Gage examined the generator. It appeared to be in working order, though its fuel reserves had been depleted. It was the kind that could run on several different sources of fuel—propane, natural gas or gasoline would all work equally well. With this discovery, my heart lifted slightly again. The computers in the labs here were on a separate server to the ones in the hospitals above. With physical access to the intact server and electricity, it should be possible to gain access to the data contained within.

Even as I thought it, I felt surprised at myself. It seemed extremely unlikely that whatever research was being performed here would be of any benefit to us, yet my curiosity refused to let me forget about it. Even before we had returned to Sécheron, I had made up my mind to petition Mercer for a tank of fuel from our stockpiles so that I could attempt to retrieve whatever information I could from the computer systems.

Beyond that, the workrooms contained stores of various chemical compounds that were of more concrete value. We loaded down our backpacks with what we could carry safely before ascending the elevator shaft once more.

Our return to Sécheron was without incident and I immediately approached Mercer with my request. He and Simon were discussing the matter of a small group of immigrants that had shown up earlier that week who had expressed an interest in joining the community. Simon's job was coordinating the scavenging efforts of Sécheron. He was also probably Mercer's closest friend.

I knocked lightly on the open door to Mercer's study, unable to force myself to wait. 'Sorry to interrupt. Have you got a few minutes?'

He exchanged a glance with Simon, who sighed and leaned back in his chair. Looking back at me, he nodded. 'Sure, Adele. Is this about the hospitals? What did you find?'

'There's some kind of medical laboratory down there, very well equipped. We managed to bring back a lot— medicine, chemicals. There's a fair bit more still to be recovered.'

Simon perked up at this. 'I'll arrange to have another group head out there tomorrow, then.'

'Splendid,' Mercer smiled at me, obviously pleased. 'It looks like you were right. Good work, Adele.'

'There's more,' I said. 'The computer systems look intact. The lab has its own backup generator. If you let me take a tank of fuel back there, I think I can get it working.'

Mercer's forehead creased. 'The notes on whatever they were working on will probably be useless to us. What do you think is on the computers?'

'I'm not sure,' I admitted. My mind raced, trying to find a justification, some legitimate reason beyond my own curiosity, but came up blank. 'It could be worth looking into, couldn't it?'

'I don't think so, Adele. It doesn't seem very prudent.' The reality was that, while we had managed to amass a significant stockpile of fuel, it was still scarce and valuable as a trade commodity. I knew that there was not a shred of evidence that wasting fuel to investigate the lab's computers would result in any sort of payoff for the community. Even so, I found myself unable to back down, compelled by my curiosity.

'Please, Mercer. There's something there, I know there is. I was right about the lab. Trust me with this, as well.'

'I thought there was a good chance that you were right about the laboratory, but odds are that there won't be anything even remotely useable for us on the computers. Even if there was, we don't have the fuel to waste on running the sort of equipment in a lab like that.'

Mercer had led our community for many years. During that time he had earned a reputation for not taking risks. I looked at Simon, but he shook his head in agreement with Mercer's decision.

'It's the smart thing to do,' I said. 'Josette would agree. If my mother was still alive, she'd be pushing for this right alongside me.' Invoking my mother's name as leverage against the man who had loved her was a low blow. It had only been two years since she had died and I knew that Mercer still grieved for her as much as I did.

His eyes narrowed. Looking over at Simon again, frustrated, he gave an angrily dismissive gesture with his hand. 'Fine.' Reaching over to his desk, he opened the drawer and pulled out a keyring, tossing it gently in my direction, 'Take some fuel. A *small* container, mind.'

I caught the keys in one hand and nodded. 'Thank you,' I said. 'It'll be worth it. I promise.'

I returned to the laboratory the next day with Madeleine, Simon and a few others in tow. While the others set about stripping the workrooms of useable resources, Maddy and I refuelled the generator with gasoline and started it. At first, it almost seemed like it wasn't going to work. The gasoline burned badly, stale and old as it was, but it had been enough to run other generators in the past.

There was a handful of seconds where I felt sick to my stomach with disappointment. However, after a minute it lurched to life and began humming along relatively smoothly. Maddy made a quick circuit of the labs, ensuring that all of the equipment and lights were disconnected or turned off, so as not to waste power, while I booted up the server.

Thankfully, the fact that the computer network was isolated from the outside world both electronically and physically had seemingly made the server administrator lax in his or her internal security precautions. It did not take long at all before I had worked out a way to access the information stored on the server through a dummy account. Once I was in, it only took a few clicks before my breath caught in my throat and my heart started racing.

Genetic engineering. Cloning. This lab had been dedicated to the alteration and creation of life. This was so outside the scope of my ability that, browsing through the data, I felt lost. Despite that, I found it incredibly difficult to pull myself away from it. I found myself captivated by what I had discovered. Only when Madeleine spoke my name and gently shook my shoulder, almost an hour later, was the spell broken.

I explained to her what we had found, but she did not seem to grasp the implications that had leapt immediately into my own mind. It was only when I had calmed down enough to explain it to her more slowly did she understand.

Our species, *Homo sapiens*, is dying. Though no one likes to talk about it, it's something we eventually all figure out or understand intuitively. An overwhelming proportion of the population burned alive when the sun scorched the planet. Many of those that survived were rendered sterile by the radiation that could now freely bombard them in the absence of an ozone layer. Food is scarce, clean water precious. Communication between settlements of survivors is unreliable, but it doesn't take much to recognise that there are fewer and fewer children being born every year. We fight to survive, to make our way in the ruins of our formerly great civilisation. Even so, there is a sense of hopelessness that permeates the struggle. It is the hopelessness of a man trapped, alive but slowly starving to death, recognising the inevitability of his fate.

This lab had been a facility dedicated to genetic manipulation and cloning. They had successfully cloned a variety of animals over a number of years, even artificially introducing genetic traits of one to another. Their last set of experiment logs dealt with a trial of human subjects.

At first, Madeleine denied me out of hand. 'It is against God, Adele,' she said. 'Man's time on Earth is done, you know this. It is naïve to think otherwise. Besides, human cloning?'

'I don't believe in God, Maddy. You know that, and if He does exist then he has long since abandoned humankind to its fate.'

'Not this again,' Madeleine sounded exasperated. God and religion were the only things we had ever argued about. We had done so quite intensely many times since my mother had died. Maddy's parents had used their faith to justify acceptance of the fate of humanity by claiming it to be all a part of God's plan and it was a trait she had inherited from them.

'Fine. Let's not bring God into it, then. Any argument against cloning lost a great deal of credibility once our species began to die out,' I said. 'What we've found…we can't simply ignore it. This is an opportunity, Maddy. An opportunity to save our species.'

'Is that really what this is about, Adele? You believe you can save humanity?'

'I can,' I said, and I believed it. Suddenly, everything about my life had clicked into place. The death of my mother, my studies—it felt as though everything up until that point had been preparing me for this. I was ready. It could be done, and I would be the one to do it.

I insisted on remaining behind when it was time to return to Sécheron. I had a small amount of food and water we had brought with us. There were printers there that could transcribe information to reams of paper a thousand times faster than I could read it. If I used it judiciously, I believed I could stretch the fuel in the generator to last a full day. I would print everything, I told her. I begged her to return the next evening with whomever she could bring with her so that we could transport it all back to my quarters at the subway station. Madeleine remained unconvinced, but yielded to my wishes. She left and I stayed behind to begin my task.

I did not sleep that day. I spent all of my time collating documents, printing all that I could find, liberating as much data from the computers as possible. There were several boxes of printer paper tucked away in a storage room, miraculously untouched by decay or mould. I used them all, filling them back up with pages upon pages of research notes and genetic theory.

I worked like a woman possessed, barely conscious of my own actions. As the printer ran off copies, I made handwritten notes copying RNA coding sequences and diagrams I found scrawled in faded marker across the whiteboards in the workrooms. I was determined to squeeze every last bit of information from the place. I took inventory of the various pieces of scientific equipment, noting down a complete list of the resources available in the laboratories in the hope that one day I'd be able to return with more fuel and run experiments of my own.

- - -

The next couple of years passed quickly. When my medical and scientific knowledge was not in immediate demand, I spent most of my free time sequestered away in my quarters, studying the material we had recovered from the lab. There was a surfeit of information, not all of it relevant to my goals. I devoured it all the same, unwilling to risk missing some crucial piece of the puzzle I was assembling. I made notes of my own, writing down questions that came to mind and noting the answers if I happened across them while I learned. Slowly, I began to construct a theoretical model of what I was hoping to accomplish.

Davin was gifted at his vocation. It wasn't too long before his mechanical expertise began to exceed that of his mentor. His skills meant that he had less and less free time, which suited me fine. Whenever he had a spare moment during the day, he would interrupt my research and we would engage in passionate, almost desperate lovemaking.

I regret that we did not have as much time to talk as would have been ideal, but we grew close regardless—I suppose we found something about each other comforting. Our relationship simply worked, without any effort applied.

Perhaps if we had spent more time together we would have discovered traits about each other that we disliked, or found each other grating or dull. The reality was that between my research and Davin's responsibilities within the community, we had only time to enjoy the gratifying aspects of each other's company. For what time we did spend together, I am thankful. Some of the memories that I look back on with the most fondness are from that time.

Madeleine remained a steadfast friend. Though she disagreed with what I was doing in principle, in practice she came to accept that my motivations were virtuous and started to believe something worthwhile could come of my work. Some of my greatest breakthroughs were thanks to her. Maddy was not ignorant of science, having picked up some degree of knowledge from me through proximity. She often spent time in my quarters as I exposited to her, acting as a sounding board and interjecting queries and speculations of her own that assisted in my own mental processes.

My younger sibling, Travis, remained enthused by my research. Whenever I faltered or flagged, frustrated by a wall I had seemingly hit or a problem I did not see an easy solution to, there was Travis. His optimism and encouragement buoyed my spirits and allowed me to pursue answers with renewed vigour. Travis and I had both undergone medical training from our mother. With my attention otherwise occupied, he spent more of his time studying her old medical textbooks. Paired with Madeleine, he deflected many distractions that would have otherwise demanded my attention. Travis treated cuts and minor injuries, only calling on me when something more serious occurred. Maddy took over the responsibilities of managing the nutrient solution that invigorated our hydroponic systems.

I returned to the laboratory beneath the hospitals several times, salvaging some small pieces of information I had missed or spending time examining the scientific equipment in order to learn how to use them. Mercer forbid me from 'wasting' any more of Sécheron's stockpiles of fuel, so I was forced to content myself with reading through the technical documentation I had found and miming the actions that would be necessary to activate the machines' functions.

Eventually, however, this was not enough. There is only so much theoretical work you can do before it becomes necessary to test the soundness of your hypotheses and engage in practical experimentation. I did what I could with what I had to hand. I harvested blood and tissue samples, using myself as a subject, and subjected them to initial testing with the limited equipment we had at Sécheron. As I progressed, more and more of my research led me to places that would require much more advanced apparatus.

I approached Mercer on numerous occasions to request fuel so that I would be able to perform my experiments, but my pleas were consistently rejected. Others in the community had begun to treat me with contempt as I withdrew further into my research. My dedication was met with derision, and I grew to resent them for it. Looking back, I can see that my single-minded focus on my work caused me to neglect my responsibilities. At the time, I was blinded by the potential of my work. I grew increasingly irate at their rejection of what I believed to be a necessary component of the survival of our species.

As my desperation grew, I recovered several empty aluminium fuel containers and secreted them away in the tunnels just outside of Sécheron. I boxed up my research and whatever necessary chemical compounds and other material I believed were necessary to my research and began the laborious task of transporting it all to the laboratory, one inconspicuous trip at a time.

It did not take long before my intention to relocate was noticed. Madeleine and Davin confronted me, cornering me one evening as I attempted to slip away with another box and a backpack full of supplies.

'Where are you taking all of that?' Davin asked.

I hesitated to respond, but Madeleine jumped in and answered the question herself. 'We know you've been creeping off each night. You're taking everything to the lab, aren't you? Why?'

'I need to continue my research.'

'You're needed here, Adele.' I could hear the concern and worry in Davin's voice. Shame welled up at the back of my throat, stifling my response. Even so, I knew I could not simply give up on my research.

'There's nothing left for you there,' Madeleine said. 'None of the equipment will work without fuel for the generator and Mercer won't let you take any from our stores.'

'I need to continue my research.' I repeated. I don't think I knew what else to say.

Maddy shook her head at my stubbornness. 'You can't live out there by yourself. It's been hard enough with the way you've been acting recently…Mercer won't have Sécheron keep feeding you if you leave.'

'There's been a small surplus since Jean and Annette died. If he does cut me off, no one will notice some rations going missing here and there,' I said, letting the implication hang plainly in the air.

'You're asking us to steal for you?'

'This is important. You both know how essential my work is. Mercer and the others, they don't understand, but you do. You trust me, don't you?' I said. I looked from Davin to Madeleine and back, hoping that the sincerity behind my words would sway them. 'Please. It'll be worth it. Trust in me, I'm begging you.'

It was then that Davin turned away from me. 'I can't support you on this one, Adele. I'm sorry. I won't try to stop you, and I won't tell Mercer anything, but I won't help you. You're obsessed.'

'I'm sorry,' I said, my voice threatening to break as his words stung my ears. I blinked away tears, struggling to maintain my composure as he walked away.

Madeleine, however, lingered. There was a sadness in her eyes, and something else that I couldn't quite put my finger on at the time. Now I think it was guilt. 'I'll help you,' she said, her voice strained and quiet. She stepped in to relieve me of the box I carried. It was then that I could no longer hold back the tears. I cried and she put her arm around me, whispering reassurances in my ear and stroking my hair.

After I had recovered myself, we returned to my quarters to retrieve more of my research material. With Maddy there, we could move twice as much in a single trip. We fell just short of being able to carry the last of it, but I had not been planning on finishing my relocation for another few days. Together, Madeleine and I slipped off down the tunnels towards the hospitals. Progress was much swifter with her assistance. It had been difficult lowering the boxes of material down the elevator shaft while on my own. With her there, I was able to lower her first before sending the boxes down one at a time.

When we had added the last of the boxes to the stack, I showed Madeleine how I intended to make use of the place. Once I had secured a source of fuel for the generator, I would keep the majority of the facility shut down and only bring equipment online when I was directly using it. The labs had provided a working place for two dozen or more medical scientists. With a full tank, the generator was designed to be able to keep the place running for a handful of days without outside power. With only me there, I believed could stretch that out to ten times as long. Attached to the generator was a battery array, ensuring that any electricity not used immediately would not be wasted.

There was a cramped room located next to the bathrooms on this level with a set of bunk beds bolted to the wall and some storage lockers. Though the mattresses were stiff and musty, they were free from mould and considerably more comfortable than the tiled floor. Past the server room I had discovered a locked utility room. After breaking in I found that, among other things, it contained what appeared to be an intact water bore similar to the one at Sécheron. Though I had not yet had time to test it, it was my hope that when the generator was fuelled the bore would still be functional. Without it, I would have to depend on water from the subway station, and the less I had to steal the better.

'I will bring you what food I can every few days. It should be enough. Let me know if you need water as well.'

'Thank you again, Maddy. You don't know how much your help means to me,' I said. When I turned to her, I took

24

a deep breath and said what I'd been steeling myself for over the past week of preparations: 'I'll need fuel as well.'

She was quiet for a moment. After a few seconds, she smiled cheerlessly and shook her head. 'I should have realised. I don't know, Adele. Mercer keeps a strict inventory of the stockpile. I can't see how we could take it without being noticed. With you moving here, it will be obvious who took it.'

'I have some empty containers. We can fill them with dirt, sneak into the stockpile during the day, while Sécheron sleeps, and swap them out. With the solar array up and running, fuel is only used when it has to be. If we put the false containers at the back end of the storage room, no one will ever have to find out. Not for a while, at least.'

Off in the darkness outside the utility room door there was a faint thud. We both froze. I rose to my feet and turned my flashlight to shine down the hall, my breathing and pulse quickening as my free hand reached for my gun. A figure stepped into the light, hands raised in front of him. It was Travis, a sheepish, apologetic smile on his face. 'Easy. Sorry, it's just me.'

'How long have you been there?' I asked, concerned.

'Long enough,' he said, gesturing for me to stop shining my light in his face. 'I want to help.'

'Travis…'

'Don't argue. I'm sick of you treating me like a kid. I can do this. Maddy, tell her.'

My gaze flicked to Madeleine, beside me. She looked back at me, her expression unreadable, before nodded slowly. 'He's right. You do treat him like a child. He's old enough to look out for his big sister when she needs help.'

They were right, of course. I had done my best to care for Travis in the years after our mother had died. After discovering the lab, however, I had been increasingly absorbed by my research. While I was otherwise occupied, Travis had seized the opportunity to prove himself capable of looking after himself. He had grown up, but I had been too busy to notice.

'All right. Thank you. Both of you.'

Together, the three of us returned to Sécheron. We went about our business until daybreak. I gathered the last of my things and checked to make sure I hadn't missed anything, Maddy cleaned the filters on the hydroponics on Platform 5 and Travis took care of a minor injury that had occurred in our absence. Not everyone slept during the day, of course, but Sécheron is a nocturnal community. With the deadly UV radiation of the solar rays bathing the city during the day, it was only natural that we avoided it and were more active at night.

Once most people had retired to wait out the sun, Travis, Madeleine and I met in a secluded spot in the tunnels. I retrieved the empty fuel containers from where I had hidden them and we filled them with dirt and mud. There were four of them, 20-litre tin containers in the same style as some I had seen in the stockpile the last time I had been inside. With the caps screwed on, it was difficult to tell that they did not contain petrol unless you deliberately shook or opened them. I knew that I'd need much more than we'd be able to take if I hoped to follow my experiments through to their logical conclusions, but it would be more than enough to start me off.

The stockpile was kept in a sealed room at the northern end of the subway complex, in what had once been an old janitorial room. Travis acted as a scout and distraction, walking ahead of us and diverting the attention of anyone we encountered between there and the fuel stockpile. He did his job well; twice we had to tread carefully as he engaged someone in light conversation. The first time, it was a woman named Lara. She had broken her arm the week prior and Travis had set the limb, so he had an excuse to speak with her.

The second encounter was trickier—a man named Adrien that Mercer often gave the unenvious job of guard duty, setting him to patrol the station during the day. Adrien was keen of sight and nervous of disposition, but welcomed the opportunity to chat with Travis as a distraction from his tedious duties. We succeeding in sneaking past without being spotted and soon came upon the door to the fuel stockpile.

It was locked, of course, but earlier that night Madeleine had requested the key from Mercer to retrieve some oil to grease the motor of the hydroponics system and 'forgotten' to return it. With luck, he would be none the wiser the next evening when she gave it back to him with an apology, even if he had the presence of mind to do another inventory check. With Madeleine keeping a lookout, Travis and I made the swap.

We snuck back out of the station and hid the containers back in the tunnels. In the evening, once it was safe to venture out, we loaded up and headed back to my laboratory. We stored the stolen fuel in an empty metal shelving unit next to the generator, then said our goodbyes.

'I will come and see you every few days,' Madeleine said, confirming what we had discussed earlier.

'I can help with that as well, if Maddy can't get away often enough.' Travis pulled me close and squeezed tightly. 'Don't go crazy out here, okay?'

'I'll try not to. Thank you again, both of you, for everything.'

Then they left me to my thoughts. I started to stow away my possessions, moving the few sets of clothes I had into the lockers in what was now my bedroom and putting away everything that was not immediately needed. My flashlight slowly ran out of power, but I did not wind it up again straight away. I sat down and the let darkness slowly close over me, leaning my head against the cool wall.

I had been so focused on relocating myself that I hadn't put too much consideration into what I would do once I had. I started to mentally weigh up how much electricity each step of the cloning procedure would require. I had been denied this opportunity for so long, it was difficult to restrain myself from forging ahead recklessly. It would be devastating to get half or three-quarters of the way through the process only to run out of electricity and have to start over. Eventually, I decided it would probably be for the best if I tested the bore first and made sure I had a reliable supply of potable water.

- - -

The next day, my preparations began in earnest. I recovered an ultrasound machine and gel from one of the workrooms and wheeled it to my bedroom, powering it directly from the generator's batteries via an extension lead. I sterilised a long needle using heat and surgical spirits, lay down on the bed, and applied a small amount of the gel to the lower left side of my abdomen before taking hold of the transducer and attempting to locate my ovary.

The machine was more sensitive to movement than I had imagined. It took me half an hour of adjusting my grip and practice just to get a reliably steady image of what I was looking for. I took up the needle and used the black and white screen as a guide as I pierced my flesh and attempted to harvest fluid and eggs from my ovary.

It hurt. My God, it hurt so much. I had been expecting pain, but had decided against taking anything beforehand because I needed a clear head to operate the ultrasound. By the time I finally was able to get what I needed the mattress was drenched with sweat, all the colour had retreated from my skin, and my hands shook so violently that I feared I would drop the precious vial of fluid.

I wanted so badly to rest, but I had only a rough idea of how long the eggs would survive once removed from my body. Hours, at least, but I needed to see whether they were viable. I did not expect them to be, but if they were I would be able to skip an entire phase of the cloning process. I cleaned my side up and allowed only as long as it took before my hands had stopped shaking before I continued.

I took the needle to the main lab and poured the fluid onto a dish, using a high-powered microscope to observe and extract the individual eggs. I already had a dish of donor cells prepared, taken from one of my tissue samples, so I began the task of attempting to transfer the nucleus from one of the donor cells to an egg. If I was able to fertilise the egg in this manner and cause it to divide, it would only take a bit more testing and experimentation before I would hopefully be able to create a viable, growing zygote.

Of course, it wasn't that simple. I hadn't expected it to be. After ruining almost a dozen eggs with my inept efforts at transferring the nucleus, I eventually succeeded at my task and settled down to wait for cell division. In the meantime, I cultured the remaining fluid and eggs, keeping them safe for my next experiment should they be required. I mentioned earlier that I had always been fairly sure that I was infertile—I had proof of that claim before the end of the day. Cell division should begin quickly, but as hours passed there was no activity from the fertilised egg.

I admit, I cried. Some part of me had still been hopeful, not fully convinced that I could never have children. Having confirmation of that fact staring me in the face was enough to make me break down for a time. I switched off the equipment and generator and spent the next few days in a dazed sort of depression as I rested and recovered my strength.

I was glad that I did, because when Madeleine came with the supplies she had promised me, she did not return alone. I heard them coming as they were lowered down the elevator shaft one by one, the number of voices alerting me to the fact that something was not right.

I prepared myself mentally as I waited, cranking the handle on my flashlight to ensure it had enough power and checking the magazine on my pistol nervously. I was concerned that if Mercer had discovered the theft of the fuel, he may try to take it back by force. I had never had to shoot a person before. I placed the weapon on a table then leant my back against it, feigning nonchalance and obscuring it from the view of anyone entering from the main doors.

It wasn't just Mercer with Madeleine, of course. The two of them came in first, followed by Travis, Davin, Gage and Simon. My brother looked anxious, but flashed a grin when he saw me. It would have been enough to put me more at ease in ordinary circumstances, but there were too many people here for me to feel comfortable. The laboratory was spacious, of course, giving me much more room than I'd ever had at the subway station. However, with so many others there I suddenly felt trapped. I believe I may have had a dash of extra nerves left over from the procedure I had given myself a handful of days earlier, as well.

'What are you doing here?' I demanded, once Mercer entered behind Maddy.

'I could very well ask you the same question, Adele,' he said. He glanced around, shining his torch this way and that to get a sense of the room. 'So this is where you've been hiding.'

'I haven't been hiding. I'm continuing my research.'

'Oh? And what have you been doing, exactly? This place is useless to you without power.' Mercer walked slowly to one side, still inspecting the laboratory.

'It's a lot quieter than Sécheron, for one, and I do have power.'

That made him flick his light over toward me. 'What?'

I swallowed, my throat suddenly dry. I've never been good at lying; it's a skill that I had never really had any cause to learn until that moment. 'I found some fuel for the generator. It isn't much, but enough that I'll be able to get a lot further with my research here than I could back at the subway station.'

'Really.' The way he phrased it, the word wasn't a question.

'I'm sorry I kept it to myself. I know I should have shared it with Sécheron, but I needed it for my experiments,'

I said. 'And I'm sorry I didn't let you know that I was leaving, but I knew you would only argue.'

Mercer was silent for a moment; he simply stood and watched me. The tension in the room was almost a physical thing—I could almost feel it pressing up against my body, trying to smother me.

'Davin,' he said at last. Mercer looked over at my former lover and gestured toward me with his flashlight. 'Talk to her.'

It was a sensible tactic. Mercer knew he could not convince me to return to the subway station on his own, so he had brought Davin in the hope that my fondness for him would erode this fixation of mine.

'Adele, what you're trying to do…I understand. I do. But it isn't possible. This lab, how many people worked here? Real scientists, people with years of training and experience. You're just one person,' Davin said. He walked toward me slowly as he spoke, eyes filled with empathy. 'You're going to burn yourself out. This obsession you have, it's going to destroy you.

'I know you want to help people, and you can. Just not here. You've got a gift, Adele, and your place is in Sécheron, using it to help people. We need you to come back. All of us.' He reached out to touch my shoulder, but I shied away. A twinge of pain from the bruised muscle in my abdomen caused me to grimace and I unconsciously covered it protectively with one hand. Davin watched in mild surprise. After a second, a flicker of understanding flashed across his face. 'You've already hurt yourself, haven't you? It's too much, and you know it. Adele, this research is going to kill you.'

'No,' I said. I straightened up and locked eyes with him. 'If I go back with you now, how long do you think Sécheron will survive? Another generation or two? What's the point of it all, Davin? What's the point in surviving if there is no future for us, or what few children we have?'

'Adele, listen to me...'

'No, Davin. You listen to me,' I looked over at the others. 'I can do this. I'm the only one who can. There is no one else.'

Davin glanced helplessly over at Mercer. The older man said nothing. Maddy cleared her throat and unshouldered her backpack, placing it carefully on the nearest table before walking over to Davin and I and taking him, gently but firmly, by the elbow. 'I think it's time for us to leave, Davin.'

'This conversation isn't finished, Adele,' said Mercer, his voice tight with anger, but he shook his head and started toward the door.

There was a shuffle of feet as people filed out of the laboratory, herded by Madeleine. Travis was the last to leave, dashing over to me before he followed them, embracing me fiercely but gently. 'I believe in you,' he whispered.

I listened to them ascend the elevator shaft, waiting quiet and motionless until the sounds of movement faded into the distance above. I cried again, after they were gone. I wished things could have been different, that the others could understand as Travis and Madeleine did. It felt like I would have given almost anything to have Davin place his trust in me, to feel his touch once more. He had said that he understood, but he had lied. How could he? If he truly understood the importance of what I was trying to achieve, that I was the only one strong enough and smart enough to

33

do it, then he would have accepted my words instead of rejecting them.

Over the following days, I continued my experiments. I had several possible ways to achieve my goal, each more difficult than the last, and, as logic would dictate, I was attempting them in order of simplicity. Access to viable eggs with high reproductive potential was something that would make the cloning process vastly faster and easier. My next step was to see if it were possible for me to use adult stem cells, extracted from my own tissue, to create viable eggs. If I wasn't able to do that successfully, I would need to obtain eggs from elsewhere.

There were two methods of extracting stem cells that I had found. While I had access to the appropriate equipment for both, neither appealed to me greatly. The first involved extracting bone marrow directly via needle. I'd read that anaesthesia was essential to this procedure, as the process was incredibly painful. I'd underestimated how much pain I'd be in when I had harvested my eggs. Extracting bone marrow sounded ten times worse. I considered asking Madeleine and Travis to do it for me, but with the memory of the last procedure still fresh in my mind I decided that it would be my fall-back option should my other method fail.

One of the workrooms contained a continuous flow apheresis machine, likely used to separate out blood samples from cloned subjects, which was perfect for my purposes. I connected myself to the machine via a cannula, inserted a needle into a vein in my arm. Blood was drawn down one tube and into the machine's centrifugation chamber, where it was processed and spun, separating out the circulating bone marrow cells. The blood was then returned to my body via the same venepuncture. I was slightly surprised at how relatively simple this procedure was, though it took half a day to collect the cells that I required.

This was when the ovary culture I had kept from my last experiment came into play. With it, I was able to successfully grow the stem cells I had extracted from my blood into new eggs. Once more, a half a dozen of the new eggs were damaged before I succeeded at transferring a nucleus. However, once I was successful, I was delighted to see the fertilisation take hold and the cells begin to divide.

That zygote was my initial proof of concept. With no uterus to nourish it, it died before daybreak, but the implication was clear: cloning was within my grasp.

My initial hurdle cleared, I began on my real work. Human cloning was central to my goals, of course, but on its own it was not the key to humankind's survival that I sought. Anytime anyone wanted to reproduce, the procedure would have to be performed, and they would be always genetic clones rather than unique offspring. There had been no logs regarding issues surrounding generation after generation of clones. However, I imagined there would be problems within such a system beyond the logistics of the science. Cloning alone was a possible solution to the death of humanity, but a messy, ill-fitting one.

Addressing the root cause of our species' decline was my ultimate goal. Through genetic manipulation, I hoped to create clones with an innate resistance to the radiation that plagues our planet, allowing them to reproduce as freely as we had in the past. A permanent answer that would allow humankind to flourish once more.

With the first stage of my experiments complete, I forged ahead with renewed vigour. I laboured over my creations through day and night, stopping only to rest when I had worked myself to the point of exhaustion. I used phenol-chloroform extraction techniques to purify and extract DNA molecules from my cells, manipulating it using the materials I had to hand through restriction digests and polymerase chain reactions. Some plants have developed natural toughness which allowed them to defy the sun's rays and so I ventured out in the night to collect samples from them. I worked at a feverish pace to create a recombinant DNA structure assembled from a combination of my own genetic material and that of the plants that exhibited the desired traits.

This took much longer than my cloning attempts. Weeks passed. Several times, I managed to accidentally destroy my work and have to start over. Madeleine and Travis took turns visiting me. Each time I expounded at length about where my research had taken me and new obstacles I had met and overcome.

My fuel supply dwindled away to nearly nothing during this time, consumed voraciously by my experiments. When I had reached a critical juncture in my tests, I realised that I would not have enough to complete my goal.

'I need you and Madeleine to get me more fuel,' I said to Travis the next time he visited. 'I'm so close. I just need a little more.'

'Of course,' he said, and smiled. 'Anything you need.'

They acquired for me a half-dozen smaller containers of fuel, propane this time, to replenish my supply. Once the generator had been restocked, I told them I was ready to begin the final phase of my experiments and bade them both to return in four or five days' time.

I used a viral vector to introduce my completed recombinant DNA into a cell culture and let it duplicate until

I had suitable donor cells. I repeated the procedure with stem-cell created eggs. Once both parts were ready, I transferred the cell nuclei to the eggs and moved them to an incubator for a few days while they began to divide and grow. Several didn't survive the process, but some did. Those that remained appeared to hold great promise.

A synthetic uterus would have been ideal, but with limited electricity and other resources, my own would have to serve. I rolled out the ultrasound machine once more to guide my hand and passed a catheter through my cervix and into my uterine cavity, using it to transfer a pair of healthy embryos into my body. The procedure was uncomfortable, but not painful.

I spent the next few days waiting, whiling away the hours by sequencing the recombinant DNA I had constructed to ensure there were no defects I had missed during my earlier trials. After I judged that sufficient time had passed, I ran the test to prove my theories had been sound. This time I was not disappointed.

At least one of the embryos had implanted successfully. I was pregnant.

When Maddy and Travis came to me as I had asked, bringing more supplies, I felt like I was about to burst from happiness. I greeted them warmly, embracing them and asking of any news from Sécheron. They seemed slightly nonplussed by my unusually buoyant demeanour. Madeleine had scarcely begun to speak before I could take it no longer and interrupted them with an exclamation. 'It worked! I'm pregnant!'

They stared at me for a few moments, shocked into silence. I smiled at them. Their expressions shifted to ones of warm joy and delight as they hugged me again.

'Will you return to Sécheron now?'

It mattered little which of them asked the question, as I knew it would be on both of their minds. 'I don't think so, not unless I need to. I do not think my presence would be welcomed,' I said. 'Besides, there is still much more to do and I can accomplish more here than there.'

Travis seemed satisfied with my response. Madeleine, however, looked less pleased. 'Davin needs to know about this. Don't you want to show him and Mercer that you were right?'

'It's too early for that. I don't know for certain if I'll be able to carry to term,' I said. One hand rested absently on my stomach. 'I have grown to enjoy the quiet and solitude, as well. I love it when you and Travis visit me, of course, but I am more comfortable here than I could ever be in Sécheron.'

'As you wish. I worry for you, though. Promise you'll consider coming back once you're further along.'

'I promise,' I said. I was surprised to realise that I meant it.

- - -

In the time that followed my appetite became ravenous. I had to ask Travis and Madeleine to bring more and more food each time they visited me, until eventually I had doubled the amount I had been previously living off.

I was six weeks into the pregnancy when I realised that something strange was happening. My body felt bloated, more so than I thought it should have at this still early stage. I had developed what I thought was some kind of periodic muscular spasm in my stomach. I feared that something had gone wrong. I brought out the ultrasound once again to check on what I could—by this time, a flickering pulse should have been visible at the very least. Once I managed to bring up a clear imagine on the monitor, however, I could scarcely believe my eyes.

Sitting there in black and white, its little heart beating strong and fast, was a fully-formed foetus. My brain kicked into overdrive. The twinges I had felt weren't muscle spasms at all. She was kicking. At six weeks. That was wrong, I knew it was. I consulted one of my medical textbooks to confirm what I thought I was seeing. It seemed impossible, but it appeared as though I was at least twice as far along as I should have been. Twelve weeks' pregnant, not six.

At first, I admit that I started to panic. The accelerated development was outside my original parameters. That meant that I had missed something when I was creating the recombinant DNA. There was even a fleeting moment where I considered terminating and starting over. Of course, my mind immediately rebelled at the idea and I rejected it out of hand. My only option was to bring the pregnancy to term. I resolved to carefully monitor the foetus' development via ultrasound. In the meantime, I spent my weeks poring over the DNA sequence of the child I had implanted myself with.

My initial projections set the term at twenty weeks, half that of an ordinary pregnancy. I was forced to revise that figure several times. During this time I grew tired and listless, as though the parasite inside me was draining all of the vitality from my body. The life growing within me began to feel more like an intruder in my body. I could not help but view its growth and effect on my own body as unnatural. Regular ultrasound scans showed the development of the foetus to be completely ordinary and unremarkable, apart from the accelerated growth. Despite that, I started to experience a sense of dread—as though there was some terrible, indescribable wrongness about what I had done.

I retained full capacity for my tasks throughout the pregnancy, though Madeleine and Travis began to treat me as though I had contracted some frailty that rendered me incapable of action. The two of them were both present at the last of my regular ultrasound examinations.

'Let me, Adele, you just lie back and relax,' said Travis, trying to take the transducer from my hand.

'It's fine, I can do it. It's a sensitive piece of equipment.' Part of me thought that perhaps I should let him, for his own piece of mind. The rest felt as though surrendering control of the instrument would be a confirmation of my invalidity.

Travis and Madeleine exchanged glances at my stubbornness, as they were so prone to doing these days, and he relented. 'Okay, but I can help if you need me to.'

I carefully rubbed the transducer through the gel, using precise motions to bring up a steady image on the monitor within seconds. I had grown quite proficient in the use of the ultrasound, so frequent were my uses of it. 'There she is,' I said as the black and white representation took shape.

'That's incredible. It's only been fourteen weeks!' Madeleine exclaimed. 'This is not normal, Adele. How are you feeling? Is everything okay? Is she healthy?'

'She's fine. We're both fine. Everything is proceeding according to my projections. The accelerated growth is expected.'

'Are you sure?' she said. Her tone was concerned and unconvinced.

'Of course.' Lying to her about it made me feel worse rather than better, but I did not want to cause either of them to worry about me any more than they already were.

'I'm going to stay with you,' Madeleine said, after I had cleaned myself up and had started to make allusions to being tired.

'That's not necessary, Maddy. I'm fine.'

'It *is* necessary, Adele,' she said, taking me by my shoulders. 'You look as though you could go into labour at any time. You need someone here. It wouldn't be right for me to leave you on your own.'

It was strange to realise that I had never actually given any consideration to the birthing process. Normally, I was so careful about planning every single step of my experiments. Even so, somehow that vital moment where I would be at my most vulnerable had managed to screen itself entirely from my mind. 'You're right,' I said. 'Of course, you're right.'

Maddy embraced me carefully, then turned to my brother and made a shooing gesture with one hand. 'Come on, Travis. Your sister needs her rest. I'll watch over her.'

After Travis had said his goodbyes and left for Sécheron, Maddy helped me into bed. She insisted on doing everything for me for the next few days, from preparing my food and bringing me water to putting me to bed when she thought I had spent too long poring over DNA sequences. It was gratifying and slightly infuriating at the same time, but I was glad that I had someone to look after me as I tried to prepare myself for what was to come.

My anxiety levels skyrocketed. I had no idea if I could safely give birth to my creation. If there were problems, what would happen? Madeleine's mother had died during childbirth. The same could happen to me. If it was necessary,

41

could we attempt a Caesarean section? As much as I loved and respected her, I knew that Maddy was not equipped to handle something like that, and I couldn't very well perform it on myself. My brother had some medical knowledge, but whether he would be capable enough to perform that sort of operation was up in the air.

After some internal debate, I aired my concerns to Madeleine. That night, she contacted Travis by radio and he returned to the laboratory immediately. Madeleine had taken up residence on the top bunk, but there were some spare blankets in the bedroom so we set up a makeshift bed for him in the main workroom.

It was that morning, after we had all retired to bed, that the first contraction came. It felt a bit like the pain I got from menstruation, radiating from my front to my back, and lasted a handful of seconds. I had not been asleep anyway, and wasn't sure it was a real contraction, so I simply lay still and waited until a second one wormed its way through my insides before I woke Maddy.

Tapping urgently on the bedframe, I called her name. She woke with a start and I could hear her sit up. 'Adele? What's the matter?'

'I think I just went into labour,' I said.

She came down and sat next to me and we talked quietly until the next contraction. She held my hand when I tensed up in sudden pain. Over the course of a few hours, the contractions steadily grew in strength and came closer together. Over Madeleine's protestations, I forced myself to stand and start to slowly walk around the laboratories, keeping only a large t-shirt to cover my body. I told her that standing and walking in early labour was much better than simply lying flat for both the baby and for myself. It would also save my bed sheets when my waters broke.

Travis joined us at some point and, after four hours, the contractions were only scant minutes apart. I barely had time to recover between bouts of fresh pain as they intensified. Unable to walk any longer, I returned to my bed. As soon as I lowered myself onto the mattress, I felt a gushing wetness as my waters broke. My body started to shiver uncontrollably, and not because of the temperature. Madeleine made sure I was comfortable as I lay back. The involuntary trembling stopped after a few minutes, coinciding with a sharp labour contraction. I cried out a little and Madeleine shifted my legs so she could check on the dilation of my cervix.

After my waters broke, it was only a half hour or so until the baby started to come. To me it felt like much, much longer. Travis was overexcited and a little panicked, so Madeleine took charge. I cried out again and again as I pushed, trying to remember all I had read about controlling my breathing during labour and having it blotted out of my mind by spikes of pain. I crushed Travis' hand in mine as I gave the final push that slid the baby's body from mine, and from down near my legs I heard a gurgling cry. With Travis's help, I pulled myself into something like a sitting position. Madeleine wiped away the blood and fluid from the child's face and wrapped her in a towel before carefully carrying her over to me to hold as it wailed.

As I lay back, clutching my creation to my chest, I felt relief wash over me. Fear over complications in the pregnancy had wound me tighter than I would have liked to admit. In the moments after giving birth, it felt like a massive weight had been lifted from my mind. At some stage someone bound and cut the umbilical cord, but I didn't notice when it happened.

Travis checked me over to ensure I wasn't having any issues with post-natal bleeding, but my body seemed to have handled the ordeal better than was expected. Not long after, I felt the afterbirth slide relatively freely from between my legs. My brother scooped up the organ and dropped it into a container for me to consume later. I'd read that in the past it had become increasingly uncommon for mothers to eat their own placenta after birth. With food as rare as it was it would be wasteful not to.

The baby quieted down after a few minutes of me holding it close to my chest, and Maddy brought one of the flashlights closer so we could see her. I inhaled sharply and struggled to pull myself into more of a sitting position, angling myself to get a better look. I had only seen a couple of newborn babies before, but I could immediately see that something was wrong. Her skin was waxy, with a slightly grey cast to it.

'What's wrong with her?' Maddy asked, and I could hear an edge of panic in her voice.

'I'm not sure. Travis!'

My brother came immediately and started to check the child over. She grumbled a bit when she was taken away from me, bursting into a fresh bout of crying a few seconds later. Her lungs and breathing were fine. Her heartbeat was strong and fast. Temperature was normal. Our initial alarm gave way to a dull sort of anxiety, but the girl did not seem to be in any sort of immediate danger. Her skin gave her a mildly unsettling appearance, like she was dead or made of soft plastic rather than flesh and bone, but without running any more intrusive examinations she seemed to be completely healthy.

'I think she's okay. I think it might just be a side-effect of her genetics,' I said.

'You said that she had developed 'within your parameters'! If that were the case wouldn't you have known about something like this?'

'It's not that simple, Maddy. DNA is a very delicate thing to manipulate. I isolated the sequences I wanted to integrate into my genetic code, but each part affects all the others. Give her some time and it may go away on its own,' I said. I think it was as much to reassure myself as it was for her.

The child started to wail again, ending the conversation before Madeleine had a chance to respond. I rocked her slightly from side to side and shushed her, and as she started to quiet down she opened her eyes. As you can see, my own eyes are blue. As she was partially a genetic clone of myself, I expected her eyes to be much like my own, and they were, but more so. Her eyes were a striking shade of azure, clear and bright like the sky in pictures from before the sun scorched the Earth.

Blinking at me, she screwed up her nose and launched into a fresh bout of howling, little hands balled into fists. The noise grated on my ears. Something about it set my teeth on edge in a way that the crying of other children never had. I was exhausted, my body drained from the ordeal it had just gone through and the fact that I had not yet had a chance to sleep that evening. I tried to calm her, becoming increasingly frustrated as she did not react to my reassurances.

'I think she might be hungry,' Travis said.

45

Madeleine took the child from me so that I could remove my shirt to reveal my swollen breasts. My nipples were slightly leaking milk, and I took the baby in my arms again and positioned her so that her mouth was near to the left one. She instinctively latched on and began to feed. She drank ravenously until the milk dwindled to a trickle and started to wail again. I carefully turned her around and placed her against my other breast and she suckled at it until my supply was completely depleted. She looked around, making small gurgling noises and weakly trying to wiggle around. Her belly had visibly swollen, full of her first meal.

After the child had settled, Madeleine asked me what I was going to call her. 'Eve,' I said.

- - -

Eve required near-constant feeding. If I was lucky, she would wait until two hours after her last meal to screw up her face and screech until I dragged myself over to her to feed her again. If I was unlucky, it would be barely an hour—my body could not possibly keep up with the demand. At least once a day, I would find myself desperately trying to shove a nipple back into her wailing mouth to squeeze out just a dribble more.

After Eve's birth, I barely slept. Her relentless hunger and ear-piercing screeches saw to that. With my body not getting anywhere near enough rest and my mind constantly bombarded with the demanding cries of my creation, the research I had been doing on Eve's recombinant DNA was forced to a halt. With my body burning itself up attempting to keep up enough milk production to satiate Eve, I found myself craving food nearly as often as she was. My brother made the trip to see us often, bringing a backpack full of food from the subway every two days or so.

In a perverse sort of way, I began to resent the child. She was the culmination of all my research, the very embodiment of my goals realised, yet at times I felt it would be a mercy to take her outside and leave her to the sun's gaze. It is a horrible thing for a mother to say, is it not? But that is how I felt. Though she was borne of my womb, of my cells and research, it took all I had to muster up even the barest scrap of motherly affection for the wailing parasite I had saddled myself with. My nerves were stretched to breaking point.

Madeleine tried several times to convince me to return to Sécheron. I stubbornly refused each time. In response, she all but moved into the laboratory, only returning to the subway station once every two or three days. When the stress grew to be such that I felt I could not bear to even look upon Eve, Maddy would look after her, allowing me to snatch what little rest I could before I needed to feed her again. It was a small comfort, but it was one I was extremely grateful for. Had I been left to look after the child myself, I don't know that I would have been able to cope.

Mercer visited my laboratory several days after Eve was born. Begrudgingly, he congratulated me on my success and finally gave 'official' permission for food to be supplied to me on a regular basis, though he knew it had been going on behind his back the entire time. He brought with him a thirty gallon drum of gasoline from Sécheron's fuel stockpile, which I believe was his way of apologising for not giving it to me in the first place without actually having to say sorry. I accepted it graciously. He did not come to see us again, though Maddy and Travis mentioned several times that he seemed to be more accepting of my situation. Apparently, he had approached them both again about me at least temporarily returning to Sécheron so that the community could help support myself and the child.

When Mercer came, Davin came with him. After that, he started to accompany Travis on every second visit or so. The four of us would talk about nothing, with the men each having a turn holding Eve at least once. Conversations with Davin were awkward, artificial. It was almost like we were strangers, learning to be comfortable with each other all over again even though we had grown up together.

My anger at Davin for refusing to support my decision to follow through with my research had cooled over the past few months, and there was a wistfulness to the way he looked at Eve and I. We started to talk privately here and there. Though we were still wary around each other, I began to think that perhaps one day we might be together once more.

'I miss him,' I confessed to Madeleine one day, Eve suckling greedily at my breast.

'He misses you, too, you know that. You can see it when he looks at you.'

'I know, it's just…' I winced a bit as Eve gummed my nipple. She had started to bite down on everything and anything she could get her hands on, making feeding her even more of a tribulation than it had already been. I was fairly sure she had started teething, but she was only six weeks old. 'I don't know. I think he wishes Eve was his child.'

'Do you wish Eve was his?'

'No,' I said, a little too quickly. Maddy looked at me questioningly and I turned away, slightly ashamed of what I'd just said. 'I mean, I don't really think of her as... she's not...'

'Adele, you—'

Our conversation was cut short as I let out a short yelp of surprise and pain. I pulled Eve away from my breast and looked down to see blood on her lips. She'd managed to take some skin off my nipple—I could see bright red blood welling up around the wound. Eve started wailing in frustration that her food source had been taken away from her, opening her mouth to reveal the tips of several teeth that had started to break through her gums.

'Are you okay?' Maddy was by my side immediately. 'Here, let me.' She reached out and took Eve from me, making soothing noises and rocking the child gently in her arms in an attempt to calm her.

I cleaned myself up, finding a small, clean cloth to hold against my breast to stop the bleeding. Eve did not stop crying, shrieking her little lungs out, and I stood there for a few minutes. I should have taken her back off of Madeleine, but I just stood and watched, bile catching in the back of my throat. I didn't want to touch her. Not at all.

After a while I fought off my revulsion long enough to thank Maddy and take the child back. She was still hungry and wouldn't stop howling, but I was unwilling to risk my other nipple in her mouth just yet. I let her tire herself out instead. Eventually, she managed to cry herself into a fitful sleep.

Eve's teeth had started to come through in six weeks instead of six months. In retrospect, it was a bit foolish of me to be surprised by this at all. The child had displayed accelerated development all through my pregnancy, growing at least twice, maybe three times as fast as an ordinary baby. Why would she have ceased simply because she was no longer inside me? It explained why she was so hungry all the time, as well—she was ready for more than just milk.

When she awoke, I was ready with some mashed vegetables. She devoured it all greedily, and almost immediately went back to sleep. You can't imagine the relief I felt. It was finally possible for me to get some actual rest, with Maddy feeding Eve while I caught up on six weeks of sleep.

That night, I had a nightmare. I dreamt I was in the room containing the lab's test subject enclosures, but it seemed to go on forever. It was dark but I could see that Travis, Madeleine and Davin were all trapped inside, caged within the cubes of plexiglass. They were panicking, pounding on the transparent walls of their cells and yelling at me, yet they made no sound.

There was something else, as well... a malevolent presence that stalked me as I ran through a maze of plexiglass, looking for some way to free my friends. I found myself cornered and, when I turned to see what had been following me, I came face to face with myself. Only it wasn't me, not really. Her skin was grey and waxy, like dead flesh. When she smiled, her teeth were like needles. Looking around desperately for a way out, I saw a knee-high tunnel through the cells. Dropping down to my knees, I practically threw myself through, crawling as fast as I could. Behind me, I could hear her closing in, her razor-sharp nails scraping on the tiled floor as she came after me.

The tunnel took me past the subject cages that held my friends. One by one, as I scrambled past, they collapsed to the ground, convulsing and grabbing at their throats, as if they couldn't breathe. Though I was moving quickly, somehow they remained where I was able to see them clearly. Their skin drew taut over their decaying flesh as they died, their bodies mummifying into ragged, skeletal things like the corpses of the two children we had found in the lab on our initial visit.

A clawed hand grabbed my ankle from behind and yanked at it, pulling me backwards even as I screamed and kicked. Around me, the mummified remains reached out to pull themselves close against the plexiglass that separated us, curling up against the barrier in a way that was almost comforting. I was pulled backwards into darkness and then suddenly there was a pressure on top of me, as through someone was straddling me. I felt her claws tearing at my throat.

When I awoke, it was to darkness and overtired, sleep-addled confusion—my mind half-convinced it was still trapped in that maze of plexiglass and death. I thrashed about, trying to throw off the imagined weight that pinned me. It took me a handful of seconds to realise I was alone, in my bed. It was only a dream, but despite reassuring myself of that fact it took what felt like hours to slow my pounding heart and calm my breathing. I did not sleep any more than night.

After that, I became a lot more settled. Without Eve constantly demanding that I, personally, look after her, I was able to start to get into something more resembling a normal routine. Madeleine and I shared the responsibility fairly equally, though I felt as though I could detect a hint of disappointment and reproval every time I seemed relieved or glad to hand Eve over to her.

Travis continued to bring us food every three or four days, occasionally bringing Davin with him. Without Eve's constant demands taxing my body, I started to return to a more normal state of being. I resumed my research, pulling apart the recombinant DNA I had forged to create Eve to better understand it. Samples I took of the child's blood and tissue held a wealth of data that I became determined to unlock. Her blood contained new compounds that only had passing resemblances to that held in the laboratory's database. My determination thusly rekindled, I set about cataloguing and analysing them.

Samples of Eve's skin showed a dense, distinctively cellulose structure, obviously inherited from the plant DNA I had introduced. I hypothesized that her greyish, dead-looking skin would grant her a similar resistance to the deadly effect of the sun's rays to that of the specimens I had tested prior to the cloning process. It was impossible to test that hypothesis without exposing her to potentially dangerous radiation and heat, of course. Instead, I filed that data away while I looked for signs that would point to whatever had caused Eve's massively enhanced growth. Only a scant handful of weeks after Eve had started on solid food, I suddenly had a dearth of activities to occupy my spare time.

I was pacing the length of the laboratory when Madeleine, in a soft voice so as not to disturb the sleeping Eve, said, 'You look lost.'

'I'm…I think I'm bored, Maddy.'

'Has the siren call of science finally ceased its wicked temptations?' she asked mildly.

I sighed. 'Realistically, there's not a lot more I can do right now. I could try experimenting with my recombinant

DNA, but really I won't know whether Eve was a success until she's a little older. Once she's hit puberty.'

'When you'll be able to test to see if she will be able to bear children.'

'Yes,' I said. A second later, I shook my head. 'I lied to you.'

'Oh?' Maddy said.

'I told you that Eve's accelerated development was something that I had deliberately caused, but it wasn't. It was a side-effect, one I hadn't been expecting. I didn't want you to worry for me any more than you already had. I'm sorry.'

'I understand.' Madeleine paused for a moment before continuing. 'In a way it's a good thing, no? It means you'll be able to tell whether you were successful sooner rather than later. Then again, you'll have less time to watch your daughter grow up.'

I looked away. 'You know I don't like it when you call her that,' I said.

'I know.'

'She's not my daughter. She is my creation. I made her.'

'What do you think a daughter is? She's your flesh and blood. She grew in your womb. You gave birth to her,' Maddy said, gently but insistently. 'She is your daughter.'

'Then why don't I feel like she is, Maddy? Why do I still resent her for the hell she put my body through? If I am her mother, I would love her, but I don't,' I said. My voice was tight and raw, and I could feel my face growing hot. 'You care more about her than I do.'

'Adele…'

'I'm sorry, Madeleine, but it's how I feel. I wish it wasn't, but it is.' My hands were trembling.

'Maybe…maybe it's time we returned to Sécheron?'

'Why?' I turned to glare at her, my tone defensive. It had been a long time since she had last made any suggestion of the sort. 'We do well enough here. There is no reason to move.'

'You said yourself that you can't do any more experiments for now. Why stay here in the lab, then? Think of Travis, having to hike back and forth constantly. He does so much for you, but do you consider how much of a burden you've placed on him? He struggles to fulfil his duties back at Sécheron as well as feed us,' she said. She walked up and took me by the shoulder, looking me directly in the eyes. 'Everyone there helps with raising children, you know that. If you truly cannot stand spending time with Eve then there will be plenty of others who will be happy to help out.

'Travis would be glad to have you back. You could repay him for all he's done. He's become a fine doctor in his own right, but he needs help sometimes and there is no one to give it to him. You said to me a while ago that you hoped that perhaps you could rekindle things with Davin. Do you really think you can do that while you hide out here?'

I didn't know what to say. The things Maddy was saying made sense. There was no logical reason for us to remain as hermits in the laboratory. In fact, it would be healthier for Eve's development if she had more people around. Still, a stubborn part of me didn't want to. I wrestled with myself over it. Madeleine could see that I was having difficulty, so she walked away to let me think. I knew it was irrational, but my mind still held onto the resentment I had built up towards Mercer and the rest for doubting me and not supporting my experiments when I had needed it.

Once I had reached a decision, I sought Maddy out and found her sitting quietly by herself in one of the workrooms. I slowly walked up to her. 'Okay,' I said. It was all I needed to say. I helped Maddy to her feet and we set about packing up everything we would take with us back to Sécheron.

The next day, Travis came with our regular supplies and was surprised to find us ready to leave. He didn't question it, hugging me and grinning after I told him what we had decided. During the embrace, I realised just how tense Travis' entire body was. It felt as though he was one giant ball of stress. It saddened me, hitting home what Maddy had been saying about what I'd been selfishly putting him through. I resolved then that I would make it up to him.

- - -

Eve's development continued to astound. She spoke her first clear word at three months old. It was her own name. She took her first few tentative steps at five months and she was walking before six. Less than a year after her birth, she began being able to string together two or three words to convey her thoughts. Pronouns confused her at first, but she learnt quickly and was soon forming simple sentences.

After we moved back to Sécheron, the rest of the community gave Eve and I a wide berth. My actions had fostered anger and resentment among the people there as their inaction had done for me. Even after some time had passed and the community had grown to accept our presence, many still held us at arms' length, unwilling to simply let go of what had happened in the past. Eve's

55

appearance did not help matters, another issue that never fully went away. Her discoloured skin, rapid growth and voracious appetite were constant reminders that she was far from being an ordinary child.

I quickly resumed my duties at the hydroponics farms. The crop platforms were Sécheron's primary source of food and there was always a slight undercurrent of paranoid that something may go wrong with them. Mercer had mandated that the crops required constant supervision, so more hands to help out were generally always welcomed.

Beyond that, Travis encouraged me to rejoin him in the surgery. I quickly learned that he had grown into a competent physician in my absence. Even so, he was still learning and knew that I was both more knowledgeable and had more practical medical experience than he. Still, I did not wish to disrupt the place he had earned himself and was content to become more of a nurse than anything else. Whenever he came to me for help, I always assumed more of a consulting capacity and let him take the lead and give the instructions.

Several weeks after the move, there was an incident. A group had been blocking off one of the subway tunnels to the south, buttressing and sealing up a dangerous section, when there was a collapse. A dozen tonnes of earth and cement crashed into the tunnel. Two people were pulverised, crushed to death almost immediately. Another was injured but was quickly dug out. The fourth was not as fortunate.

I mentioned Adrien before, I think. We didn't know he was still alive. After the tunnel had collapsed, he found himself protected by an arc of concrete that had fallen above him. He was able to crawl out, squeezing through gaps in the rubble, until he made it to the surface. When he tried to climb out, the debris shifted and settled. He was pinned, trapped where no one could hear his cries for help.

It was only the next night, when Davin and a few others ventured onto the surface to inspect the damage from above, that they found him. You've seen someone who's been caught in the sun, I take it? The deep, angry-looking burn of a mild exposure. The terrible radiation sickness that comes after spending more than a handful of minutes in direct light. The way skin starts to blacken and peel. The smell is the worse thing, I think. That awful, sickening stench of burning flesh and hair.

Adrien had been out all day. Sunrise to sunset. He had been roasted, skin flayed from his flesh to expose the blackened and charred muscle and sizzling fat beneath.

Afterward, Davin came to the surgery with an injured forearm. He had it bundled up in a towel, blood soaking through. 'Christ, Davin! What happened?' I said as I rushed to him. Travis had stepped out to run some errands, so it was just the two of us.

He told me what they had found and how he had climbed down to pull Adrien free so they could bring the body back. 'Made a stupid mistake,' he said. 'Cut myself on a torn rebar.'

'Idiot.' I took his arm and carefully unbound the wound to get a better look at it. We had little more than strong antibiotics to deal with tetanus and similar conditions. Injuries like Davin's were a serious matter. It was bleeding profusely, but it looked clean and relatively shallow. 'You're going to need some stitches,' I told him.

'Oh, good.'

I set about cleaning the wound, using warm water to wash the area before bringing out some rubbing alcohol.

Davin hissed through his teeth when I applied it, but remained still and let me work. My hands were steady and moved with surety—an advantage gained from having had to perform numerous surgical procedures on yourself was that you are forced to learn a speed and accuracy that could not be gained anywhere else.

I stitched the wound closed and applied a bandage to ensure that the bleeding would stop, and then cleaned up the mess I had made. 'There,' I said. 'You'll be fine.'

I retrieved some antibiotics from the locked medicine cabinet for him. 'You need to be more careful, you know. I should think I would be very cross with you if you took ill,' I said. When he didn't reply right away, I touched him gently on his unhurt arm. 'Are you okay?'

'Yeah, I think so,' he said. 'It's just…it was awful, Adele.'

I didn't know what to say. Instead, I leant in and put my arms around him. He nestled his face in the crook of my neck and we stayed like that for a few minutes.

Davin's body felt warm and strong beneath mine. Holding him like that stirred something in me I had not felt since before I had left Sécheron to perform my experiments. When the embrace finally ended, I was hesitant to let go of him. As I lingered close to him, I found myself unable to resist leaning down and brushing my lips gently against his.

Davin's eyes widened in momentary surprise, but then his hand snaked around the back of my neck and he pulled down at me eagerly, his lips and tongue questing hungrily over mine. I kissed him back, harder and stronger than I ever had before. Before I realised what was happening my clothes were coming off, my hands seeming to move of their own volition as they stripped me bare and pulled my naked body

58

close against Davin. His body was warm and hard and he smelt of sweat and dirt and motor oil. I ached to feel him inside of me again.

- - -

Sécheron hosted a small party for Eve when she turned two. This wasn't unusual. We had always made such a big fuss over birthdays for the children. They are so precious now that the celebrations were a good way of reminding ourselves just how thankful we were to have the few that we did. It was around then that she had started to make proper friends with some of the others. By then, she looked and acted more like a four or five year old child than anything else. People had even begun to grow used to her unusual appearance.

The day after, I had just finished testing the nutrients level of the solution that fed the hydroponics system and was headed over to see Travis at the doctor station when I saw Eve, sitting at the top of one of the broken, old escalators. She was staring down at the level below and didn't move as I approached.

'Simon doesn't like me,' she said as I drew closer. She didn't turn to face me.

I peered down past her and could see that she was looking down at Mercer, Simon and Gage as the three men pored over a map of Geneva. I couldn't make out what they were saying, but I knelt down beside Eve and put an arm around her. It was meant to be comforting, but I felt awkward. 'What are you talking about? Of course he likes you.'

Eve leant her head against me and continued to stare. I don't think she blinked once. 'He doesn't. He told Mercer I was bad.'

'You're not bad.'

When I said that, she looked up at me. Her eyes seemed even bluer now, clear and bright and full of intelligence. 'Del doesn't like me either.'

Del was what she called me. 'Of course I do,' I said, pulling her closer. She hugged me back, but didn't say anything else. 'I'm going to see Uncle Travis. Do you want to come?'

Eve looked back down at Simon, a thoughtful expression on her face. A few moments later, she looked up and nodded quietly.

A tension had risen in my chest when she had looked at me and told me I didn't like her, and didn't loosen until long after I put her to bed that day. Were my feelings toward Eve truly that obvious, that even she could tell? I had thought I was doing a reasonable job of playing the parent, but that was apparently not the case.

Eve hit puberty not long after she turned four. It sounds alarming when I phrase it like that, but at the time it seemed perfectly normal. Her growth rate varied somewhat, but was usually in the vicinity of two or three times that of a normal human. Girls usually start puberty anywhere from ten to fifteen years old, so it was within expectations.

It was around that time that Simon burst into Travis' surgery, looking as though he had just run a marathon to get to us. 'Both of you, quickly! There's been an accident!'

When we arrived, it was to find Lara sitting on the floor nursing the head of her nine-year-old daughter, Jeanette, a small pool of blood at her side. The child's skin was deathly pale. Her mother was holding a cloth soaked with crimson against her forearm. Simon and Lara had both heard Jeanette scream and found her lying on the ground with her arm broken, the bone visibly jutting from her flesh.

'Did anyone see what happened?' Travis asked Simon as I knelt beside Lara, unshouldering my medical kit.

'I don't think so,' he said. 'I think she might have fallen.'

'It's going to be okay, honey,' I said soothingly, placing my hand on Jeanette's forehead. Her skin was cold and clammy with sweat. She didn't respond to my words, though her eyes showed that she was still conscious. Her body was wracked with trembling and her breath was coming in short, weak gasps. I checked her pulse. It was weak. She had clearly gone into shock.

'Please, do something,' Lara pleaded with me.

'First we need to elevate her legs. Simon, can you help Travis?'

'Of course.'

Together, the two men slowly and carefully lifted the child's legs and slid Travis' medical kit underneath. I looked at Lara. 'You're going to need to let her lie flat. Someone get something to cushion her head, but we need to make sure her brain and organs are getting enough blood.'

While that was happening, I coaxed Lara's hand away from her daughter's arm and lifted the cloth to reveal the wound. As far as open fractures went, it was a particularly nasty one. Her radial bone had snapped and one of the jagged ends was poking out about two centimetres above the skin. I covered it again to continue to staunch the bleeding as my mind considering the injury. Open fractures are difficult to deal with without access to a proper surgical theatre.

Without knowing exactly how she'd hurt herself I wasn't sure about the full extent of the damage yet.

'We need to get antibiotics into her,' Travis said next to me. 'If that gets infected she could die.'

I nodded. 'It should be safe to move her, if we're extremely careful. We don't want to aggravate the soft tissue damage, but we can't treat it here. We need to get her to the surgery.'

Travis grabbed Simon by the shoulder, pulling him away so that they could run to fetch a stretcher while I monitored Jeanette's condition. Something nagged at the back of my mind about the injury, as well. Simon had said that they thought she had fallen, but the bruising I had seen around the fracture looked more consistent with her arm getting caught underneath something and snapping from pressure. I took a vague look around while we waited the long minutes until the men returned, but couldn't see anywhere nearby where she might have caught her arm.

Travis and Simon returned and we carefully transferred her to the stretcher. Lifting her was nerve-wracking. I remember thinking that she felt so light, as if she weighed almost nothing. As soon as she had been set down in the surgery, Travis was inserting a needle into her hand, attaching the tube to a bag of clear antibiotics. We scrubbed our hands and forearms clean then put on surgical gloves. Once we were prepared, we set about debriding the wound, cleaning it of dirt and foreign material before cleansing and irrigating it with several litres of saline solution.

I injected Jeanette's arm with a small dose of ropivacaine to numb the pain—with an open fracture like that, I would need to reposition the bone fragments into their normal alignment and screw them together. At some stage, she passed out. Travis and I panicked a little when it happened, double-checking all of her vitals, but she hung on, pulse and breathing remaining weak but stable as we worked. There were no further complications with the surgery. Once we had finished, Travis bound up her arm tightly to prevent her from moving it.

After cleaning myself up and disposing of the bloodied gloves, I stepped outside to find that a small crowd had gathered in the cramped passageway. There was only a scant dozen children in Sécheron at the time, so one being hurt this badly was a serious matter for the entire community. The air was thick with apprehension. Simon had been leaning against the wall near the door, his arm around Lara and her head on his shoulder. They both immediately moved toward me as I exited the surgery.

'How is she? Will she be okay? Can I see her?' Lara's eyes were red and puffy, her cheeks streaked with dried tears.

I nodded. 'With luck, she will be fine. She's not awake, but you can go in and see her if you would like.'

'Thank you, Adele! My poor Jeanette…'

The crowd started to disperse, the oppressive tension dissipating into relief as people went back about their night. While Lara sat in the surgery beside her daughter, Simon turned to me and nodded. 'I know we don't see eye to eye on a lot of things, but I want you to know that I do respect you and the work you do. Thank you.'

'It's what I'm here for,' I said.

Simon nodded and went into the surgery after Lara. I sighed and stretched my neck, the muscles still tense from performing surgery.

'Is Jeannie gonna be okay, Del?'

I jerked back, startled. Eve had only spoken softly, but somehow she had managed to get right in front of me while I was distracted by my stretching. The sudden closeness had caught me off-guard. By this point in time, she looked slightly older than Jeanette was. 'She'll be fine. Travis and I looked after her,' I said, composing myself.

Eve didn't respond. She simply stared at the door to the surgery with her piercing blue eyes. Eve and Jeanette played together sometimes, so it made sense that she would worry after her friend.

'She's resting now, but you can see her later.' Reaching out, I put my hand on Eve's shoulder and steered her away from the door. 'Come, now. Shall we get you something to eat?'

'Okay.' Food was always a good bet with Eve. The one thing that had remained constant with her was her unceasing appetite. In a day she'd often eat as much as Madeleine, Travis and I combined.

It was the next evening, after Jeanette had recovered enough to talk about what had happened, when Simon came to see me again. I was visiting Davin in his workshop. There had been a fault with one of the battery banks for the solar panels, causing an acid leak that did some damage before it had been noticed. Gage and Davin were carefully cleaning the acid residue from the batteries and determining what was still usable and would need replacing.

Simon stormed into the room, flinging the metal door open with a loud clang. I turned to face him, alarmed. 'Keep your little experiment away from my family,' he said, voice tight with anger.

'What are you talking about?' Behind me, Davin and Gage stopped work.

'Jeanette's arm. It was her.' He took a threatening step toward me and gestured sharply with his hand. 'If that freak goes anywhere near her again, so help me...'

Davin stepped past me, placing a hand on my shoulder as he did, and put himself between me and Simon. 'I don't know what you think Eve did, but just take a step back and we can talk about it.'

Simon's face turned red and he opened his mouth to say something, but stopped. He took a deep breath to calm himself slightly and leant back against the cool cement of the wall. When he finally spoke, it was in a more even tone. 'Eve and Jeanette were playing yesterday. Jeanette said that she broke her arm.'

'What? Why would she do that?' I asked, trying to keep the defensive edge out of my voice.

'You tell me. I never liked that...that *thing* you created. She's not right.'

'Don't call her a thing,' Davin said.

I touched him gently on the back. 'It's okay. Simon, I understand why some people might not like Eve. She's different, but she's still just a little girl. I'll talk to her, ask her what happened. I'm sure it must have been an accident.'

Eve was surprisingly strong for her size and slight build—it was something that had already caused me no little amount of concern. I'd examined her carefully and it seemed as though her tendons were thicker and stronger than that of an ordinary child of her age. Because of her rapid maturation, as well, she had little time to become accustomed to being a given size or strength, making her quite clumsy at times.

'Do whatever you like,' said Simon, shaking his head. 'Just keep her away from Lara and Jeanette.'

I'd worried about Eve's strength a little, but I hadn't really thought about the possibility that she might accidentally hurt someone else. It was important that I resolved this quickly and tried to head off any fallout we might suffer. Simon had Mercer's ear and he and Lara were both well-liked in the community. If they started blaming Eve for their daughter's injury, sentiment could easily turn against the both of us.

I found Eve at the surgery with Travis. He had taken out the skeletal anatomy model that our mother had used to teach us and was talking about bones and their structure while she listened intently. Travis grinned at me when I interrupted, but I shook my head in return and sat down next to Eve.

'Eve, honey, we need to have a talk,' I said. 'About yesterday. Is there something you want to tell me?' I waited for a response, but Eve just stared at the floor. 'Simon had a talk with Jeannie and she told him it was you that broke her arm.' Eve sniffed and looked up at me, tears welling up in the corners of her eyes, but didn't say anything. 'Eve, tell me what happened.'

'Ease off a little, Adele. She's upset,' Travis interjected, hunkering down in front of her. 'It's okay, precious. I know you mustn't have meant to hurt Jeannie, but you've got to tell us what happened.'

'Jeannie was teasing me,' she said. 'She kept saying I was a test tube baby. I told her I wasn't but she wouldn't stop. I got mad. I didn't mean to hurt her.'

'You should have stayed with her and told us what happened,' I said. 'Jeanette was badly hurt. She could have died.'

'I was scared!' she sobbed. Travis leaned forward and put his arms around her, letting her cry into his shoulder for a little. When the tears had mostly subsided, she pulled her reddened face away from him and looked up at me with puffy eyes. 'I'm sorry, Del.'

Luckily, Simon and Lara weren't overly vocal about the incident, but it still became common knowledge fairly quickly. What had happened between Eve and Jeanette put a damper on our relationship with the rest of the community.

Travis didn't let it affect him at all. Any time Eve was upset because of being excluded or overhearing something said about her, he would hug her and tell her that the others just didn't understand how special she was. People trusted him more than me, too, meaning they were more likely to go to him in his capacity as a doctor, and more likely to not give him a hard time about it.

- - -

Not too long after the incident with Jeanette, Eve had her first period. It seemed normal, as I'd hoped, and I rushed to take her on an expedition to the laboratory where she had been created and born. Travis and Madeleine came with me, and we used some of the fuel that Mercer had given me to generate enough power to run the ultrasound machine. We ran a battery of tests and at the end of it, I was ecstatic. Everything indicated that Eve was fertile.

The satisfaction of knowing that I had been successful in my endeavour, that I had been right to pursue my experiments, tempered the sickness I felt in the pit of my stomach every time I saw Eve. I still felt uncomfortable around her, but the resentment and disgust that had plagued

67

me since I had become pregnant had eased to a level I could ignore.

The rest of Sécheron remained coolly civil to us, reaching a natural equilibrium where we were tolerated but not made to feel welcome by most of the community. There were exceptions. Davin and I were spending time together regularly again, despite the pressure on him to turn his back on his relationship with me. Maddy and Travis continued to help look after Eve where they could. It felt as though the two of them were much closer to her then I would ever be. Watching them, it would be easy to imagine a casual observer mistaking them for her parents.

Travis continued to teach Eve about medicine and anatomy, mirroring the lessons our mother had given us when we had been growing up. She devoured the knowledge whole, learning everything he could teach faster than he could teach it. I soon added heightened intellect to the list of traits that my recombinant DNA had brought out in her.

At six years old, Eve appeared to be in her early to mid teens. She looked more and more like me as she matured, though her facial features were a little sharper, her eyes were still that intense shade of blue and her skin remained a pallid grey. Her hair grew thick and lustrous and, where I liked to cut mine short to keep it out of my way, she asked to wear hers long.

We should have told her about her origins at some point. At the very least, we should have had a plan for when she started to ask questions about why she was so different to everyone else. We weren't keeping it a secret from her— nothing like that—it was just an awkward topic to raise and we kept putting it off. She worked it out on her own, eventually. When she did, she confronted Travis about it and he brought her directly to me.

'I know what I am,' she said to me, her face defiant.

'And what is that?' I asked mildly.

'An experiment. You experimented on me.'

'You sound angry.'

'Of course I'm angry!' she said. Frustration and disbelief tinged her voice. 'Look at me! What did you do to me?'

'I made it possible for you to exist,' I said. Putting down the book I had been reading, I folded my hands in my lap. 'I couldn't have children of my own. Not many of us can. I made a choice for the survival of our species.'

'What did you *do* to me?'

'The laboratory in the university hospitals at the southern end of the city—I took you there a few years ago. Do you remember it? It used to be dedicated to research into genetic manipulation and cloning. I used it to create you. You grew from my body.' I stood up and stepped over to where she stood. She flinched slightly as I raised my hand to touch her cheek. 'But you're more than that. I didn't want to just clone myself—that would have been pointless. You're different because I changed your DNA. I made your body tougher, resistant to the radiation that is slowly killing the rest of us.'

Eve pulled back from my hand and looked away. 'You made me a freak.'

'You're not a freak,' I said, mustering what conviction I could.

'Listen to yourself, Del. You don't even believe it.'

'You're not a freak,' said Travis, his voice much firmer and sincere than my own. He took Eve by the shoulders and forced her to look him in the eye. 'You're not. You're my niece. Don't pay any attention to what the others say about you. Whatever they say, it's because they're afraid because you're different. There's nothing wrong with being different.' He put his arms around her. Eve sunk into his embrace and squeezed back, burying her face in his shoulder. At first I just stood back and watched, but then Travis shot me a look and I stepped over as well, putting my arms around them both.

We remained like that for a few minutes until Eve lifted her head from Travis' shoulder. 'I want to see it,' she said.

'See what?'

'The lab. Where you made me.' Eve extricated herself from the hug and looked at both of us. 'I remember going there before, but I didn't *know* then. I want to go there again and see where I was born.'

'Why?' I asked. 'There's nothing there.'

'I just want to. Please?'

Travis looked over at me. 'I don't see the harm in it,' he said. 'We could go tomorrow.'

'Alright. We'll head out tomorrow evening. I'll let Maddy know where we're going.' I looked back at Travis meaningfully. 'It would probably be better if we didn't tell anyone else.'

The three of us headed out the next day. It had been a long time since I'd last visited the lab. Even so, I still knew the way almost instinctively, following the subway tunnels as far as Genève station before emerging to cross the dried-up bed of the Rhône into the southern half of the city.

Scuttling through the darkened streets, the weak beams of our wind-up flashlights playing over the decaying buildings, we came across a small scavenging party from Les

70

Charmilles, ranging far from their home. We greeted them warily, ensuring our weapons were close to hand should we need them. The two groups exchanged news of their respective communities and, afterward, they offered to trade some of the things they had found. We declined and excused ourselves. The tension we had felt eased off as their lights faded away into the distance and we continued on to our destination.

At the hospitals, we returned to the outbuilding that housed the elevator shaft down and secured our climbing equipment. It felt comforting, somehow, to come back to the lab. Having spent as much time as I had there, it felt like something of a homecoming. The big steel doors, once a nigh-impassable barrier, were coaxed open once again with a crowbar and we were inside. The place was dusty, but untouched—it didn't seem as though anyone else had been down there.

Stepping lightly over to the far side of the room, I waved the beam of my flashlight over an area of floor. 'Here,' I said. 'This was where I gave birth to you.'

Eve was quiet, walking between the tables of scientific apparatus. Her eyes swept over everything, taking it all in. I continued on, illuminating each piece of equipment that had contributed to her creation and explaining what it did. This is the apheresis machine. This is the centrifuge. This is the ultrasound. As Eve went along behind me her fingers trailed along beside her, lingering on the surface of each in turn, but she remained silent. Awkwardly, I continued to go over the process that had led to her birth, describing each step in detail in an attempt to fill the conversational void.

'What's in this room?' Eve finally spoke as we wrapped up her tour of the facility. She was standing near the door to the subject containment room.

'Nothing. Just ghosts,' I said. After I had moved into the laboratory, I had kept the room full of plexiglass cells sealed up, even going so far as barring the door to reassure myself that there was nothing in there that could harm me.

'I want to see.'

A bout of irrational fear gripped my chest when Eve insisted on seeing the room. The dream I'd had years ago about it and Eve leapt vividly into my mind as though I'd only just woken from it. I swallowed the dread, letting it settle in my stomach like an iron ball. 'Okay.'

Travis removed the wrench I'd used to jam the door shut and the two of them disappeared inside. I lingered at the door, trying vainly to control the fear that threatened to overwhelm me. It had just been a dream. Eve wouldn't hurt me. Travis was there to protect me. After a few minutes, I summoned what willpower I had and tentatively followed after them.

Travis turned his head slightly to look at me as I came up beside him. His expression was one of mild concern, but he said nothing, simply nodding his head in Eve's direction. She lay on the ground, perpendicular to the walls of a row of cells, her flashlight lying discarded next to her. Her body was curled right up against the plexiglass. As I took a step closer I could see the desiccated remains of the two children inside the cells illuminated by the slowly-dying light.

She lay there like that for a time. I'm unsure exactly how long. It felt like an age, each minute dragging on and on, every second struggling to pass. Travis and I simply waited— it did not seem right to interrupt. However long we stood there, it was long enough for Eve's flashlight to run down. The bodies of the children faded into the darkness and Eve slowly pulled herself into a sitting position. She turned to look back at Travis and I, the indirect light from our own flashlights reflecting off her eyes. 'What's going to happen to me, Del?'

'What do you mean?' I asked.

'I grew up faster than everyone else. Will it keep going? Will I get old really fast as well?'

I didn't answer right away, but when I did, I was honest. 'I don't know.'

'You don't know?'

'Growing up and getting old are two different processes,' I said. 'Just because you matured quickly doesn't mean you'll age any faster than a normal person once you're fully grown, but I can't say for sure either way. You growing up so fast was a side-effect of the recombinant DNA—it wasn't something I made happen intentionally.'

Eve turned back to the dark cells in front of her, leaning forward a little to rest her head against the plexiglass. Travis and I stayed quiet and eventually she stood up. Bending back down to pick up her flashlight, she wound the crank on it briskly for a minute before looking over at us. 'We can go now.'

We moved in subdued silence, exiting the laboratory and wedging the steel doors shut behind us once more. We headed back into the elevator and climbing through to its roof, picking our way through the chunks of cracked and fallen concrete. Eve was the first to ascend. We had brought climbing gear and it was a simple matter for us to use the ropes and pulley to lift her to the surface. Once she was safely above, Travis turned to hand me the rope.

I shook my head and pushed his hand away. 'You go next,' I said. 'I want a moment by myself. I don't think I will ever come back here.'

'All right,' Travis nodded and clipped the rope to his climbing harness. Travis was a lot heavier than Eve, but she was as physically strong as he was. Between her pulling from the top and me helping at the bottom Travis was lifted to the top in a few minutes.

Stepping carefully over the top of the elevator, I dropped down and walked back into the short concrete hallway. The glow of my flashlight had started to die out, so I cranked the handle until it shone brightly again.

I walked back to the double doors that blocked access to the lab. Reaching out with one hand, I touched the brushed steel with my fingertips. The metal felt cool and solid, impassive and unyielding yet somehow reassuring. Unintelligible words filtered down to where I stood—Eve and Travis were talking, but I could not hear what was being said. I ignored them, focusing on the door and what lay beyond it.

Had the months I had spent locked away in there been worthwhile? Maddy and Travis would say it had. Without my experiments, Eve would never have been created and I knew how much they loved her. It remained to be seen whether Eve truly was resistant to the radiation that was killing humanity. Even if she was, would she be capable of bearing children that would inherit that genetic heritage? There were still many questions to be answered. Until they were, I could not decide whether my stubborn pursuit of science had succeeded in giving our species the spark of hope for survival I had so desperately sought or whether it had all been for nothing.

A sharp cry of alarm startled me from my reverie. My veins turned to ice a second later as the sound was followed by the loud, hollow bang of something hitting the top of the elevator. Sprinting the short distance to the elevator, I scrambled up through the roof, my heart pounding. There was a weak rasping breath next to me and I brought my flashlight around to find Travis lying sprawled on the uneven metal, splayed at a visibly unnatural angle.

'Oh God, Travis!' Dropping to my knees next to him, I dumped my flashlight off to the side, angling it so I could still see. My hands were shaking. I didn't know what to do.

'Adele…'

'Don't speak,' I said. 'It'll be okay. You'll be okay.'

I frantically searched over his body, careful not to touch him, and came upon the jagged point of a broken metal rebar protruding two inches from his abdomen. Judging from the way his body lay arched and the presence of the rebar, he had landed directly on the fallen pieces of concrete that littered the top of the lift. There was little chance that he had not broken his spine. I felt a sticky wetness start to soak through the knee of my trousers and my eyes filled with tears. There was nothing I could do for him.

Travis tried to say something else, but the words didn't quite make it out. A ghosting of pink bubbles frothed at the corner of his lips as his mouth worked soundlessly. I leant down to carefully rest my hand on his collar, taking his hand in mine and gently resting it against the side of my face. I could feel his heart beating, fluttering like a trapped butterfly. 'Travis, I'm sorry. I'm so sorry. I love you.'

Next to my head, the barely perceptible rise and fall of his trembling chest stopped. I could no longer feel his pulse.

I started to cry in earnest then, great heaving sobs wracking my chest. Tears flowed freely, my face and eyes burning as my entire body shook. My little brother had just died in my arms. Grief clouded my mind. It took some time for me to bring it under anything remotely resembling control.

I slowly lifted my head from Travis' collar. My vision was blurred and I was glad that I did not need to look clearly upon his dead features. His eyes were open and I closed them with trembling fingers. Sitting up, I breathed deeply a few times, trying to calm myself. A fresh wave of tears threatened to erupt and I buried my face in my hands, trying to blink them away. My throat was raw from sobbing, aching at every shuddering breath.

I rubbed at my eyes with the back of my sleeve and retrieved my flashlight from where I had dropped it. My hands, covered in my brother's blood, shook so hard that I almost dropped it again. Slowly rising to my feet, I looked up. Though distant, I could make out a silhouette looking down the shaft toward me. Eve. She had done this. After all Travis had done for her, all he had put himself through to help look after her, this was how she repaid him. She murdered him.

No. It was *my* fault. Eve was my creation. I had murdered Travis. My mind and body had both rejected Eve, fearing and resenting her since the moment she had started growing inside me. Now I knew why. I should have known better than to ignore my own instincts. Something somewhere inside of me had known all along. She was never the second chance for humanity that I had thought she would be. She was a monster. It had been staring me in my face this entire time and I had refused to see it, refused to acknowledge that my experiments might have created something more horrible than I could have imagined.

There had been warning signs. I had ignored them. Even discounting my own bias against her, she had never seemed quite right. The incident with young Jeanette, too, should have alerted me to her true nature. Again, it was Travis who had defended her then, who had protected her when I had confronted her about what she had done. He loved her as if she were his own and she betrayed him. She betrayed all of us.

I screamed at Eve, a wordless cry of grief and rage and hate that scoured my already-sore throat. I shrieked at her until my insides seized up and the scream was stifled by the contents of my stomach as I doubled over, retching. At some point I lost my flashlight. My entire body trembled violently. I crawled on my hands and knees through the blood and vomit to drop down into the elevator.

My knee hit the ground hard but I ignored the sharp pain that shot up through my leg, scrabbling over the floor into the hallway towards the laboratory. Wedging my fingers into the small gap between the doors, I heaved at them with what strength I could force into my limbs. They shifted only slightly. I tore at them in a frenzy, my grief and fury-addled mind oblivious to the fact that Travis had deliberately jammed the doors shut when we had exited the lab.

Somehow, I managed to claw the gap open just enough to fit my head through and I jammed myself between the doors, desperate to get inside. My body was wracked by a wave of sobbing. I whimpered quietly to myself as I struggled and contorted my body in an effort to worm my way into the lab. Inside, I crawled forward through the darkness until one of the tables loomed in front of me. I pulled myself underneath it, huddling in the back corner and curling into a ball.

- - -

I don't know how long I stayed there, barely moving, staring sightless off into the black. I cried and shook until my body simply couldn't take any more. I sunk down and let the darkness claim me as I drifted off into a nightmare-haunted sleep. I woke several times. My lips became cracked and dry, my raw throat parched and painful. My stomach churned, demanding sustenance. All of it barely registered in my mind. I soiled myself at some stage, my body attempting a desperate protest against remaining where I was, but still I did not move.

When the light finally came, it burnt my eyes like fire. I would have cried out in surprise and pain, but my body was simply not capable of making more than the barest squeak of noise. My memories past that are confused, disjointed, but I will relay what I can of them. Strong arms wrapped around me and pulled me from my hiding spot, firm and warm, lifting me into the air. I was blinded by the glow of flashlights, though when my eyes began to adjust I saw familiar faces around me, Davin and Madeleine and others. They were talking but the words didn't make any sense to me.

I remember being carried down the hallway outside the laboratory, toward the elevator. When my mind realised that I was being taken back towards where Travis had died, to where Eve had murdered him, I panicked. I began struggling against the arms that held me, weakly kicking and flailing. I parted my lips to speak, to will myself to talk. 'No,'

I tried to say. 'No please don't take me there. Travis, oh God, Travis. No no no no no nononono…' But my throat choked on the words, suffocating them before I could let them out, leaving nothing left but a low whimpering. If I had had the strength to fight back properly, I would have been hysterical.

I must have passed out after that, as I do not recall being taken up the elevator shaft or the return to Sécheron. I remember gradually easing into consciousness, aware of the feel of clean linen against my bare flesh. My entire body ached, as though someone had taken a sledgehammer to every inch of me. I felt light and heavy at the same time and dimly realised that my insides were screaming at me for food and water.

Opening my eyes felt as though it took a Herculean feat of effort. My surroundings slowly swam into focus as I peered between my barely-separated eyelids. I lay in my own bed, back at Sécheron, in the room that Travis and I lived in. The room was darkened, but the door was open and light filtered in from the corridor outside. A motionless shape sat silhouetted in a chair between the bed and the door. As my eyes adjusted, I could see that it was Davin. He was leaning back in the chair, eyes closed, obviously dozing.

I tried to sit up and winced as every muscle screamed at me, forcing me to stop and lie still until the pain subsided. Opening my mouth, I licked my chapped lips. 'Davin,' I said in a quiet rasp. Eyes focused on my lover, I raised a trembling hand to try to reach out to him. My fingers brushed the material of Davin's pants but I could do little more than rest them there, unable to summon the strength to grab hold of him. Exhausted by the effort it had taken me to move even that little bit, I closed my eyes to rest and drifted back off into unconsciousness.

I found myself back in the hallway outside the laboratory, but it was different. The lights were on, fully powered, and the doors and concrete lacked the scars of age and damage that marked them. It was as it would have been, back when the lab was operational.

Across from me there was a melodious tone, signalling the arrival of the lift. I turned to see who would emerge, but the doors did not open immediately as I expected. Dark crimson began to seep from the seams in the doors. I started to back away. A curtain of blood oozed over the metal, covering the door completely. I continued to step backwards, fear catching my breath in my throat, and the doors slid open.

A pool of red spread from the elevator, spilling out of the blood-soaked interior. Inside stood a lone figure, completely covered in blood as though she had been utterly immersed in it scant moments before. Turning, I sprinted the last few metres to the laboratory doors. They opened as I approached, welcoming me inside, then slammed closed behind me with a resounding clang.

The interior of the laboratory was brightly lit, faceless men and women in white lab coats scurrying about here and there, operating the equipment and working on computers. When I say 'faceless', I do mean literally—each scientist had a completely smooth oval of skin where their face would otherwise be. I wandered down the middle of the room, casting anxious glances back the way I had came. The small windows in the metal entry doors were completely black, as though nothing lay beyond but empty void.

Without warning, vice-like hands closed around each of my biceps and started to roughly push me forward. I cried out in surprise and alarm, tossing my head this way and that to catch a glimpse of my assailants as I fought against their grip. Two of the female scientists had taken me by the arms and were pushing me toward one of the other workrooms. They were incredibly strong and despite my struggles I could not free myself.

The doors slid open at our approach and I was ushered inside. The room we entered was not as I was expecting. Instead I was presented with a perfectly white room set up as an operating theatre, several faceless nurses in scrubs laying out implements and apparently preparing for a surgery. The operating table in the middle of the room was covered in restraints such as those you would see in a hospital's mental ward.

When I realised what was to happen next I began to flail about again, wrenching at my arms to try to break their grip. My efforts were wasted. They threw me onto the table, one grabbing my shoulders and pinning me to its surface while the nurses swarmed over me, strapping down my ankles and wrists with the restraints. I screamed at them, over and over, but they ignored my cries of protest.

Somewhere toward my feet I heard the sound of doors sliding open again and lifted my head to see. My view was blocked by my pregnant stomach, as full and round as the day before I had given birth to Eve. As well as being pregnant, I was also suddenly completely nude. I was stunned into silence by the sight of my swollen belly, ceasing my struggles. As I lay there, Travis walked up beside me, clad in a white lab coat the same as the others. He put a comforting hand on my belly and smiled at me. 'There, there, Adele,' he said. 'It will all be over soon.'

I stared at him mutely as he gestured to one of the faceless nurses. She handed him a scalpel from the tray of surgical instruments and he began to cut, slicing a long incision along my belly as though preparing to gut a fish. It didn't hurt, feeling more like someone was dragging a pen across my stomach, but I screamed anyway. Travis ignored me and continued to work, using the scalpel to cut through the subcutaneous fat beneath my skin. With the gloved fingers of his free hand, he pushed the gelatinous yellow fat aside to expose the fascia, and nicked it with the scalpel. He offered the bloodied implement to a nurse, who replaced it with a pair of surgical scissors.

Travis used the scissors to methodically snip open a long gash across the fascia. I could feel the blades tugging at my flesh but found myself paralysed with fear, unable to fight what was happening lest his hands slip. Craning my neck, I watched in horrified fascination as he exposed my abdominal muscles and then pulled them apart to reveal the next layer, the lining of my abdominal cavity. After he cut through it, the nurses around me started to hook the edges with metal retractors, pulling the flaps of tissue open and holding them there to expose my internal organs. Even straining my neck, I could not see Travis' hands any longer. Too much of my opened body blocked the view. Still he continued to cut, slicing through the final layer and then laying open my uterus.

Travis stopped and turned to drop the surgical scissors on the tray of bloody implements, then looked down at his handiwork. His mouth split into a wide grin and he reached into me with both hands, taking hold of something solid and lifting it. As his hands came back into view, I could see that he was taking Eve out of me—not as a baby, but impossibly fully-grown. He had taken hold of her head and was pulling her, naked and encrusted with blood and amniotic fluid, out of my body. She shivered as her shoulders came into view. Reaching up, she wrapped her arms around Travis' neck as he continued to pull her free of my body.

Once her feet slid wetly from inside me, Travis backed up and angled himself so that Eve could stand next to him. She held on to his neck, resting her head against his chest, the blood and fluid covering her body staining his lab coat. Travis looked back over at me and smiled. 'Look at her,' he said. 'Isn't she beautiful?'

'Travis,' I stammered weakly, reaching out toward him with one hand. 'Get away from her!'

Eve let one of her arms slide down from Travis' neck to the metal tray of surgical implements. Almost lazily, she fingered the handle of the scalpel that he had just used to cut me open. He didn't seem to notice, right up until she took hold of the scalpel and thrust it, hard, into his side.

Travis let out a gasp as the blade plunged into his flesh, a patch of red rapidly blossoming on his coat where she had stabbed him. Eve stepped back and he collapsed to the ground, his body folding beneath him like a marionette that had just had its strings cut.

I heard the door slide open again and Madeleine stepped into view. 'Maddy…' I said. 'Run, quickly, get out of here!' I tried to warn her, but it was like she couldn't hear me or see Travis' body lying at her feet. Eve beamed at her, spreading her arms as though inviting Madeleine to embrace her. Maddy stepped forward, returning the smile and bringing her arms up to wrap around the monster's waist. As

Maddy came within reach, Eve's hands came down to take hold of her jaw. With a single, smooth motion, she broke Madeleine's neck with an audible popping sound.

Eve slowly stepped back over to where I lay, bending down slightly to look me in the eyes. 'I didn't mean to hurt them,' she said, her tone mocking. 'It was an accident.'

There was a flicker of movement in my peripheral vision and then Davin was there next to her. 'She's a monster,' I said desperately, trying to get his attention. 'She's a killer.' As with Madeleine, however, Davin acted as though I wasn't even there, putting his hand on her shoulder in a fatherly gesture.

Eve reached out to gently touch his chest with her fingers. Crimson began to well up where she touched him and she pushed her fingertips through his flesh as though it wasn't even there. Davin collapsed, joining Madeleine and Travis on the floor. Eve turned and wordlessly presented me with his heart. Staring at the bloody organ, I tried to pull at the restraints binding me to the table. It was a futile effort and Eve laughed at me as I struggled, dropping Davin's heart on the ground next to him. She reached into my still-open abdomen and started to grab hold of my organs, ripping them out of my body one by one with gleeful abandon. I screamed.

There was an instant of vertigo and then I was lying in my bed in Sécheron again, disoriented, my eyes flickering open in a sudden jolt. I must have made a noise as well—Maddy was in the chair by my side and she jerked forward as I returned to consciousness. 'It's okay, Adele,' she said in a soothing voice. 'You're all right, I'm here.'

Speaking required effort that I wasn't sure I could summon. Even so, somehow I managed to croak out the word 'water'.

Madeleine nodded and reached down, her hand disappearing out of sight momentarily to return with a plastic bottle of water. She unscrewed the cap and leaned in to me with the bottle. 'Here.' Lifting the bottle to my lips, she let a trickle of water dribble from the bottle. I raised my head slightly and drank what I could. The water was cool and delicious, but stung my raw throat on its way down. I choked and coughed at the unexpected pain and Maddy took the bottle away until I managed to compose myself. 'Are you okay? How are you feeling?'

I winced and gave my head a small shake. 'Hurts. All over.'

Madeleine touched my hand gently. 'Don't talk. You need to recover your strength. You haven't eaten in over a week.' Replacing the cap on the water bottle, she leant down to place it back on the floor. 'I started to worry when you didn't come back. It was two days after you left that I went to Davin and Mercer and we came looking for you.

'We found Travis…' Turning her head as she trailed off, she blinked several times and wiped away the tears under her eyes. 'Eve is still missing. We found you under a table in the laboratory. You were dehydrated. We gave you water when you would swallow it, but most of the time it was like you were catatonic. There were a couple of times where you seemed to be awake, but you didn't understand what was happening. You were incoherent. We thought… we thought you might die.' She paused for a moment, her eyes searching my face. 'Adele, what happened?'

'Eve,' I croaked. 'Killed him.'

'But that doesn't make any sense. Why would she do that?'

Shaking my head, I felt my face grow warm. My vision blurred as the tears came again, hot and wet, and I began to sob. It hurt, but I didn't care. Travis was gone. He was dead because of me. My own arrogance had led me to create the monster that murdered my brother.

Madeleine made shushing sounds and moved over to sit on side of the bed. Leaning down, she draped her arms around me in an embrace. 'I'm so sorry, Adele. Travis was…' she trailed off. I could tell from the ragged way her chest moved she was crying as well, though she was trying hard to stifle it. We lay there for a time, each strengthened by the comforting presence of the other in our mutual grief. After we had finished crying, Maddy straightened up. 'I need to go let the others know you're awake,' she said. Her voice was strained. 'Do you think you could manage to eat something? We can mash up some vegetables for you.'

I nodded, a tired but grateful smile on my lips. 'Thank you.'

Maddy squeezed my hand for a second before she got up to leave. Looking back down at me for a moment, her forehead creased in concern. 'Once you've recovered a bit more we can talk about Eve.'

- - -

The next few days were spent recovering my strength. Davin and Mercer came to see me not long after, obviously dropping whatever they had been doing once Madeleine told them I was awake. I managed to choke down some vegetable mash and drink a bit more water. At first, anything I put in my stomach threatened to come back up again, but I managed to keep it down.

The two men bombarded me with questions, Davin almost crushing me in a tight embrace as he warned me never to make him worry about me like that again. Eventually Maddy had to usher him away. He wouldn't leave my side willingly, but she knew that after the effort of eating my body would need more rest to process it and begin recovering.

As with my pregnancy, it was Maddy who took it upon herself to look after me during my recovery, ensuring that I ate and drank enough and pushing me to exercise my weakened muscles. In the week or so I had spent catatonic, my body had depleted its fat stores and started attacking itself in search of nutrients to keep me alive. With Maddy's help, my strength began to return, slowly but steadily. It took a couple of days before I could reliably manage to leave my bed without assistance and even then my atrophied muscles were barely able to support my own weight.

'Are you okay?'

I was asked variations on that question a lot during the next month. Every evening when I went to break my fast in the mess someone would look at me, say 'Hello' and follow it up in the next breath with 'How are you feeling?' as though, each day, they expected the answer to be something other than 'Fine'. Every time someone happened upon me sitting by myself, occupied with my own thoughts as I stared off into the distance, it would be 'Are you alright?' or 'Is everything okay?' even though they knew I wasn't and that things weren't.

Davin would call on me often, but our conversations were halting and awkward. More often than not, we would end up staring at each other in silence. He did not let that dissuade him, however, even though I expected him to get frustrated, to stop wasting his time coming to see me. Davin seemed to intuitively understand what Travis' death had done to me. The only time he seemed to so much as acknowledge there was something wrong with me was the pity and sadness that would glide across his features whenever he thought I couldn't see him.

As the days passed, I became more and more taciturn toward the other members of the community. I began to neglect my duties at the hydroponics farms, but no one dared to say anything to me about it. Mercer, especially, I would have expected at this point to have been the least likely to tolerate my antisocial behaviour and yet he seemed to be making sure I would get all the space I needed while I grieved.

In spite of all of this, no one seemed to grasp that it was more than just grief over my brother's death and Eve's disappearance that plagued me. I felt like I had failed in the worst possible way. I hadn't just failed myself or Travis, I had failed everyone. Davin, Mercer, Gage, Lara, Jeanette, Simon, the rest of Sécheron, the rest of the whole of the world. Everything I had done up until that point, everything I had done to save the world, to save humanity, was all for nothing. I had set out to create hope for the future of our species, to fight against the bleakness and misery that pervaded what was left of our God-forsaken planet. Instead I had created a monster, a creature that had brought us nothing but fear and death.

Maddy came across me when I was preparing to leave. I was cleaning my pistol, leaving it lie in pieces across the bed that had belonged to Travis as I worked, when she walked into the room. Her eyes flicked toward the backpack on my bed, full of food I had manage to steal from the common store and other supplies. 'Adele, what are you doing?'

'Leaving.' I did not look at her.

'You're being foolish. What are you talking about? Leaving for where?'

'Just… leaving,' I said. I began to reassemble the gun with precise, practiced motions.

I felt a hand on my shoulder and Maddy pulled me around to face her. Concern was painted across her features, her brows knitted together in worry, the corners of her mouth downturned. She shook her head slightly. 'No. You're not well, Adele. I don't know where you think you're going, but I won't allow it.'

'I can't stay, Maddy,' I said. 'Here, this room, Sécheron. It's too much. I can't go on like this. I need to be alone for a while.'

'You need to be here, with people that love you, so we can look after you.' Maddy put a hand on the pistol and gently tried to take it from me, but I did not let go. 'You're not thinking clearly. You just need some more time.'

'Time and space. We grew up here, Maddy. Every corner of this place holds his memory. If I stay, I'll see his face everywhere for the rest of my life. I need to be away from here to clear my head.'

'Then I'll come with you,' she said.

'Maddy…' my vision blurred, my eyes filling with tears. 'No. You've always been here for me. You've done so much that I will never be able to repay. Words cannot express how grateful I am to you, but this is something that I can't ask of you. I need to be by myself. Please understand.'

Madeleine released her grip on the gun and embraced me fiercely. I hugged her back, squeezing as tightly as my still-weakened body could manage. When she pulled back to look at me again, her face was red and she was trying not to cry. 'I don't understand, Adele.' She let out a short, sad laugh. 'I don't think I have ever really understood you, but I believe in you. I trust you. And I love you.'

'I love you, too,' I said softly.

'Okay. Okay, then.' Maddy wiped her face on her sleeve and then gave me a tight smile, 'You're leaving. What do you need? How can I help?'

'I'm already packed and ready. I leave today, at noon, while Sécheron sleeps,' I said. 'Don't tell anyone about this conversation. Not even Davin. As far as anyone should know, I disappeared during the day without a word.'

Maddy's mouth opened. It seemed as though she was about protest, argue that I should reconsider, but she stopped, closed it again and nodded. She squeezed my shoulder one last time, her eyes searching my face, then she turned and left.

That day I crept away, disappearing into the subway tunnels and making my way to the station at Genève. The tunnels past there had collapsed long ago, so it was as far as I could go until night fell. I exited the station a bit sooner than I should have, the dying embers of the sun cast long shadows over the city. I had a long way to go and I wanted to make sure that I could make it before daybreak. The moon and stars were bright enough to see by, but I had my flashlight with me as a precaution.

I headed west, out of the city, toward the mountains. Trepidation rose in my stomach with every step, each moving me further away from the safety of Geneva's crumbling infrastructure. I had lied to Madeleine about why I was leaving, about what my real intentions were. Of course, had I told her the truth she would have done anything to stop me. I would have been put under lock and key by Mercer and Davin 'for my own good'.

There was nothing left for me. I loved Davin and Maddy, but I hurt them too much. My existence did nothing but cause pain and grief. I was a burden on them and on Sécheron. I had caused strife in the community, stolen from people who had trusted me and given them nothing in return but failures. My intention was to head to the mountains and ascend to the highest point I could on Le Reculet, or perhaps Le Crêt de la Neige, and find a good vantage point. There I would wait, my eyes covered by the most heavily filtered darkened lenses I had been able to find. I would bear witness to something which had once brought beauty and comfort to the world, but was now little more than a portent signalling the death of our species—I would watch the sun rise. And then, I would put my gun in my mouth and pull the trigger.

I followed the road, passing up through Meyrin and Saint-Genis. After the first few hours my feet were already hurting. I ignored their protests and pressed on. At Sergy I turned south, searching for a way up to the mountains. I was prepared to cut across the burnt woods if necessary, but I knew I'd make better time and be less exhausted if I could find a proper route. The map I'd brought with me was aged and partially illegible, which was more than I could say for the cracked and burnt faces of the hauntingly blank street signs that tried vainly to direct me. By midnight, I had pieced together enough to find Rue de Reculet, the road that would lead me up the mountain, and was steadily advancing upward.

It was eerily silent, out there in the wilderness, further from Sécheron than I had ever been before in my life. The air was still but cool. My footsteps seemed to carry far off into the night. As I walked I tried to picture what it would have been like before, when green grass grew over the hills and copses of trees dotted the countryside. Illuminated by the brightly shining moon and stars, the bare, sun-scorched earth was replaced in my imagination with a beautiful landscape, teeming with birds and animals. I imagined the road trembling beneath my feet as convoys of cars and trucks rumbled along the bitumen and smiled to myself in the darkness.

Eventually the road gave way to a dirt track and I took out my flashlight so I could watch my footing as I hiked up the mountainside, following trails that had seen no human footprints for decades. The sun-hardened trunks of the dead trees I passed stabbed at the night sky like dark knives, the last defiant reminder of the vegetation that had once flourished here. I stopped several times to drink from one of the plastic bottles of water I had brought with me, discarding the container and leaving it behind once it was empty.

As I began walking again, I heard a faint sound, like dirt crunching underfoot. Silent as the night had been so far, the sound seemed incredibly loud to my ears. I froze, ears straining to listen for any sign of further noise. Slowly, I turned on my heel and cast the light of my flashlight out over the dark mountainside. Seconds crawled by, agonisingly slow, but eventually I convinced myself that my mind had played a trick on me and I turned to continue up the mountain.

'Del?'

The voice was quiet, but unmistakeable. My hand went to the grip of the pistol at my side as I turned toward the source and I drew it to point at Eve, standing less than a dozen feet to the left of the trail. Her eyes reflected the illumination from my flashlight oddly, glinting yellow and green, but she did not flinch back from it or the weapon in my hand. She was wearing something long, tattered and brown draped over her, a makeshift hooded cloak made from sackcloth.

'Eve…' My throat had gone dry and her name came out as a hoarse whisper. The hand holding the gun trembled, but I kept it trained on her.

'I missed you,' she said. I didn't respond. 'Where are you going?'

I stayed quiet, frozen in place, until she took a step toward me. 'Stay back! Don't come any closer!' I lifted the pistol to aim at her chest, trying to steady my grip.

'Del, please,' Eve said. 'I just want to talk.'

'Talk, then,' I said, my voice quavering and uncertain.

'I…what happened with Travis. I never meant to hurt him. I'm so sorry,' her voice wavered. She almost sounded on the verge of tears. 'It was an accident. You have to believe me.'

Despite myself, I found the barrel of the gun and the circle of light from my flashlight slowly lowering to point at the ground near Eve's feet. Anger and grief welled up inside me and I took a deep breath to try to slow my beating heart. 'You killed him.'

'I know.'

'Why?'

'I loved him,' she said. 'It was wrong, but I thought…I was always so lonely. I never had any friends, no one to grow up with or share anything with. Travis was always there for me. I thought that maybe…' she trailed off.

I felt like she had punched me in the gut. My mind raced, almost unable to comprehend the words. She and Travis had always been close, but something like this had never crossed my mind. It horrified me that she would have felt like that toward him. He had practically raised her, alongside Maddy. He was like a father to her. I stood there silently, dumbstruck, as I absorbed the revelation.

'There was no one else around. You stayed below in the lab. It was just Travis and me. I tried to kiss him. He pushed me away, told me to stop. I didn't want to. I thought that if I held on, that if I could just make him taste me, touch me, that I could make him feel for me what I felt for him. So I tried harder. He kept pushing me, and…'

'Stop,' I said. 'That's enough.' I could taste bile rising in the back of my throat. Over the past month, I had often dwelt on Travis' death, trying to puzzle out why Eve would have kill him, to ascribe a motivation to the senseless act that had been committed. Now I knew. The pieces clicked into place. There was no doubt in my mind that Eve spoke the truth.

'I can't come home, can I.' Eve's voice was timid, but the sentence was more of a resigned statement of fact than a question.

'No.'

'No one would believe me.'

'I don't think so.'

'They hated me already. They were always scared of me.' She sounded frustrated and on the verge of tears. 'It's not fair. I loved him, too.'

'I know.'

'I don't want to be alone, Del. Please don't leave me out here all alone.'

I looked down at the pistol in my hand, mind filled with a sudden clarity of purpose. 'I won't,' I said. 'I promise.'

'Del! No!' Eve's eyes went wide as she saw me lift the gun toward her again and she ran at me. She grabbed my wrist just as I squeezed the trigger. The gunshot split the night air with a loud crack and then I was falling backwards with her on top of me. We hit the earth hard and the air was driven from my lungs. Eve easily wrestled the gun from my grip, my weakened body barely an obstacle to her unnatural strength, and then threw the weapon off into the darkness.

A spatter of blood dripped down onto me. Looking up at her face I could see that the side of her head was bleeding. The bullet had grazed her. 'Del,' she said, her voice quavering. 'I'm so sorry. I don't want to die. Please. I don't want to hurt you.'

I lay there beneath her for a few seconds, my breath coming quick and sharp, before I weakly pushed at her. 'Let me up.'

She hesitated for only a moment before complying, rising to her feet and offering me her hand. I took it and hauled myself up, putting as much of my weight on her as I could. She barely seemed to feel it. We stood there for a few moments, watching each other.

'I want to live, Del, but I don't want to be alone,' Eve said, her tone soft. 'You made me. Make me a friend. A companion. So I don't have to be alone.'

I shook my head, 'No. No, I can't.'

'You can. Look at me, Del. I'm alive. I'm a person. You made me. I'm your responsibility. Don't I deserve a chance at happiness, same as anyone else?'

'You could go somewhere else. Away. Find another place with people who will accept you.'

'There isn't such a place, and you know it. People are afraid of things that are different to them. I'm sick of everyone being afraid of me. Make me someone else, someone the same as me,' she said. There was desperation, a sense of urgent misery, in her voice. 'You won't have to carry him. Make a boy using an egg from you and put him inside me. You won't have to raise him. Once he's born I'll take him away from here. We'll go away. We'll leave forever and find somewhere with no people, so we can live in peace.'

'I don't…' I trailed off, disgusted and confused. Eve's proposition repelled me. I understood her desire not to be alone, to have someone to share her life with, but the incestuous solution she had come up with disturbed me to my core. Yet I could not think of any other satisfactory answer.

Eve was right. There was no way she would ever find a community that would accept her without reservations. They would distrust and fear her. There would eventually be some incident as there had been with Travis, she would flee, and the cycle would repeat itself. She was right, too, in saying that she was still my responsibility. I was the one who created her Through that bond, I was responsible both for her actions and her future. After what had happened with Travis, the very idea of tolerating her presence, of taking her back into my home, horrified me. Yet I still needed to be held accountable and do what I could to mitigate the damage my own actions had caused.

'Del, please…'

I turned my head, averting my gaze from her. I could not stand to look in her eyes. 'Okay,' I whispered. 'Okay. I'll do it.'

- - -

We made good time on the return journey, though the awkward tension between us stifled any possibility of the time passing quickly or comfortably. Eve accompanied me as far as Genève station before we split up. She headed south, towards the old university hospitals and the laboratory beneath, while I re-entered the subway tunnels and made my way north. My return coincided with that of a small expedition led by Simon, scavengers out combing the ruins for things of value to the community. I used their arrival as a distraction to slip in through a disused side tunnel.

Once inside the station, I dispensed with stealth and set a brisk pace as I headed toward the hydroponics farms. It was around this time, just before morning, when Madeleine was inclined to perform a final check of the farms for the night. Heading down to the platforms, I spotted her on one of the catwalks overlooking the crops and started up the metal stairs toward her. She heard my clanging footsteps as I approached and turned toward me. I could see her eyes widen slightly in surprise and she stopped in her tracks.

'Adele?' she closed the last few paces between us herself, stepping forward to embrace me. 'You've been gone all night, I thought…'

'So did I. There is something we must discuss in private. Can you come to my room once you're done here?'

'I can come now, if you'd like?' she said.

'You have time to finish up here. I have something I need to do first.'

Maddy nodded, smiling at me, before she turned back to her work. I exited the room as swiftly as I'd entered it and headed toward my next destination.

When Sécheron had been a functional part of the subway network, the maintenance area at the northern end had been used if one of the subway trains had had a malfunction and needed to be pulled off the main tracks. There were some secondary tracks that could be used to take a carriage to the depot at the far end of the subway line, but in a pinch minor repairs and maintenance could be performed at Sécheron itself. The equipment that had been already at the platform plus the ample space had meant it was the ideal site to convert to a machinist and electronics workshop. It was where Gage and Davin, along with a small handful of others, were based.

I found Davin putting away some tools in a rusted red cabinet. He looked up as I came over and grinned. 'Hey, beautiful,' he said. 'What brings you down here?' It had been a very long time since I had last come to visit him, rather than the other way around.

I smiled back and brushed his lips gently with mine as he straightened up. 'Just checking up on you. I want you to come to the surgery so I can take a sample of your blood.'

'What for?'

'This was pretty nasty,' I said, reaching out to touch the scar on his forearm. 'You haven't shown any signs of anything being wrong, but I just want to make sure that you hadn't picked up any infections. Since Travis died…I just don't want anything to happen to anyone else I love.' I knew that Davin's experience with medical matters did not extend far beyond the simple first-aid training that all members of the community were given, so it was unlikely he'd know that there wasn't any need or way for me to test his blood for infections. It hurt to lie to him, even more so to invoke Travis' name so that he wouldn't ask any questions.

However, I knew that if I told him the truth there was no way he would ever agree to what I was going to do for Eve.

'All right.' A sympathetic look flashed across his face at the mention of my brother and he nodded. Turning back to the cabinet he closed the door and slid the padlock into place, snapping it shut. 'I'm done here. I was just about to turn in for the day anyway.'

Davin followed me to the doctors' surgery. I sat him down in a chair and wrapped a blood pressure cuff around his bicep. Inflating it, I checked the vein running down the inside of his elbow and swabbed the area with iodine to disinfect it. Using a needle and catheter, I half-filled a blood bag from his arm.

'That's it,' I said, withdrawing the needle and covering the hole with a cotton ball to stop it from bleeding. 'Hold onto this for a minute.'

Davin caught my hand as I went to turn away, catching my attention with his eyes. 'I love you,' he said.

I smiled. 'I love you, too. Give me a second. I need to put this in the fridge.' I scooped up the blood bag and took it over to the small medical refrigeration unit in the far corner of the room. The surgery was one of the only places in Sécheron with easy access to electricity from the solar cells for luxuries like refrigeration. I wasn't too worried about bacterial proliferation in the blood sample. All I really needed were some intact cells from Davin to use as a template for the cloning process. Even so, I did need to make sure that the blood survived long enough for me to transport it to the laboratory.

Once the blood was away, I went back over to where Davin sat and used a bit of tape to stick the cotton ball to his arm. That done, I leant down and kissed him. He kissed me back, gently at first, but then with increasing insistence, his tongue slipping into my mouth. My heart quickened in my chest and I could feel the heat rising in my cheeks as he stood and put his arms around me, one hand at my waist and the other behind my head.

My body responded instantly, leaning in to the kiss without thought, a sudden wetness growing between my legs. We hadn't made love since Travis' death. My grief had eclipsed any interest on my part and Davin would never dream of pushing me if I wasn't completely comfortable, but now I ached with desire for him.

He pulled back so he could look into my eyes and then, in unspoken agreement, we moved toward the door as one, our hands tugging at each others' clothes. The door to my room was open, the lamp by the bedside casting illumination into the corridor. Neither of us realised the room was already occupied until Maddy rose to her feet as we stumbled in.

There was a second of awkward silence as she took in our flushed faces and partially undone clothes. Her face lit up in what was probably the biggest smile I had ever seen her wear and she hurried past us and out the door, pulling it closed behind her. Davin and I looked at each other and laughed before renewing our assault on each others' clothes.

Davin and I spent the entire day making love. When I finally stumbled out of bed to clean myself up it was already early the next evening. We said our farewells, Davin returning to his workshop while I went out in search of Madeleine. I found her at the mess hall, breaking her fast. Grabbing some food for myself, I joined her at her table.

'I'm sorry about yesterday,' I said. 'I wasn't planning for that to happen.'

'You don't have to apologise. I'm glad you and Davin are intimate again. After you left I was afraid you were never going to come back.' Maddy smiled at me wistfully. 'It's nice to have someone you can be with like that.'

'It is. You should start seeing someone. I can't even remember the last time you spoke to me about boys. You spend so much time looking after me...I'm sorry if it's been difficult to have your own life as well.'

'I was seeing someone, until recently,' she said. Her voice was quiet. Sad.

'You were?' I asked, looking at her questioningly. 'You never told me about it. I don't remember ever seeing you spending time with anyone, either.' Madeleine was my best friend—I shared everything with her. It shocked me a little to realise that something had been going on with her and I hadn't even noticed.

'It doesn't matter. What did you need to talk to me about?'

'Not here,' I said, looking around. 'Come back with me after we finish eating.'

After we'd finished our meagre breakfast and washed our dishes, Madeleine and I returned to the surgery. Once I was satisfied that we were alone, I outlined my encounter with Eve, being careful to omit anything that might cause her to suspect the real reason I had left the subway station. After I was finished she simply sat there quietly, absorbing the implications of what I had just told her. 'I think I have to go through with it,' I said. 'She's right. I owe her that much, don't I?'

'I don't know. Give me a minute.' Maddy shook her head. There were tears in the corners of her eyes, 'Eve was in love with him...'

'Are you okay?'

She nodded, wiping her eyes with the back of her hand. 'Yes, I'm fine. Okay. You're going to clone yourself again?'

'Not me. Davin. Eve wants a male companion. I never looked into what would be involved in swapping the gender of a cloned embryo. It would be possible, but I'd have to research it and the sooner we get this thing done, the better.'

'He'd never agree to such a thing.'

'He'll never need to know,' I said. 'I've already taken a sample of his blood. It should be enough.'

Madeleine stared at me, her expression suddenly sad. It took her a few seconds to speak again. 'I'll help you, but this is the last time, Adele. I won't keep lying for you. I can't.'

I turned away, finding myself unable to meet her gaze. We left for the laboratory the next evening, packing what little supplies we would need and some food for Eve. The tunnels were quiet and we made good time through the darkened city streets as we made our way to the hospitals.

I paused as we approached the elevator shaft, my stomach lined with lead. The last time I had been there, my brother had died in my arms. Inside my mind, I pictured Travis and Eve arguing at the open doors of the elevator, her trying to kiss him and him pushing her off with both hands. She was stronger than he was and he stumbled backwards, his foot finding only empty space behind him. Eve reached out to grab him, misery and surprise painted across her face in equal measure. Her fingers touched only air and he fell, plunging down into the blackness.

Shaking my head to clear the images, I took a deep breath and unshouldered my pack, busying myself with the ropes and climbing equipment. There was no sign of Eve. She said she would meet me at the laboratory but, as far as I knew, she didn't have any gear to make the descent safely and hadn't been lurking at the top waiting for us.

Once below, the dirty brown stains of Travis' blood demanded my attention, brusquely shouldering their way into my vision every time I moved my flashlight, no matter how hard I tried not to see them. To escape them I disconnected myself from the ropes and dropped down into the elevator far quicker than was safe. Madeleine followed closely behind.

'I was starting to think you weren't coming.' Eve's voice turned the blood in my veins to ice as we entered the main workroom. My flashlight glinted off her eyes unnervingly as I moved it to locate her, sitting in a chair near one of the desks at the side of the room. 'Maddy?' she said, sounding vaguely surprised. 'What are you doing here?'

'Adele asked for my help.'

Eve stood and took a few tentative steps toward her. 'Its…good to see you again.'

Madeleine didn't respond. Hefting the container of fuel that I had brought with me, left over from the gift Mercer had brought me after Eve had been born, I broke the tense silence. 'We need to get the generator running. Hopefully this will be enough for what we need.'

Her gaze lingering on Madeleine, Eve nodded slowly. 'Just tell me what to do.'

We reconnected the smallest of the lab's refrigeration units and I retrieved Davin's blood sample from the Styrofoam cooler we had transported it in, separating it into several smaller sterilised containers and storing all but two for later. Many years had passed since the experiments that had created Eve. Even so, I fell back into my old work routines fairly quickly, as though I had never been away at all.

I used the extraction method I had perfected during my initial attempts at DNA manipulations to purify and extract the requisite molecules from Davin's blood. That done, I manipulated their structure with restriction digests and polymerase chain reactions to the specifications recorded in my notes. I lost track of time, absorbed in my own little world of recombinant DNA and modified genetic structures. It only took a day and a half for me to successfully replicate the changes I had made to my own DNA to create Eve.

Madeleine returned to Sécheron once or twice, making sure we weren't overly missed and stocking up on more rations to leave with Eve during her pregnancy. I worked myself to exhaustion, refusing to take more than a couple of hours rest before forging ahead. Having two extra pairs of hands helped speed preparations when it came time for the next stage of the process. Equipment was sterilised and the ultrasound machine was rolled out. Guided by its flickering black and white images, I inserted a long needle into Eve's abdomen to retrieve the required eggs from her ovaries.

Leaving her in Madeleine's care, I busied myself with the next phase, using a microscope to separate out a cluster of cells ready for the nucleus transfer. Distractingly, Eve appeared at my elbow as I began the process of attempting to successfully transfer Davin's genetic material into the ova without damaging them. I managed to ruin three eggs before I chased her away with a glare and a few curt words. Once I had a handful of successful, healthy embryos, we transferred them into Eve's uterus via a cervical catheter.

'Is that it?' Eve asked, once I had powered down the ultrasound.

'That's it.'

'Oh.' She sounded almost disappointed. 'I just thought it would be more…complicated.'

'It took me a huge amount of research and dozens of experiments to even approach this point. You're only seeing the end result, the culmination of years of work,' I said. Packing away the last of the equipment, I headed to the server room to power down the generator. 'We'll be back in a few days so I can run a few tests to confirm whether any of the embryos managed to successfully implant.'

'You're just going to leave me here, alone?'

I turned to look at her, my expression hard. 'Is that a problem?'

'I just thought that maybe…no. Never mind. I'll see you in a few days, then.'

We left without another word. Madeleine and I ascended to the surface, hurrying to spend as little time in the elevator shaft as possible as we passed through it. Once we had made it outside, I touched her on the shoulder. 'Thank you. Your part in this is done.'

Madeleine responded with a nod of her head and turned to leave. She paused for a moment to look back at me. 'Those procedures…you did all of that by yourself? To yourself?'

'I had already asked so much of you and Travis,' I said. 'It was something I thought I had to do on my own.'

She leant back against the wall and looked up at the sky. It was a clear night, stars and nebula glimmering like shining jewels painted across the heavens. Maddy sighed. 'I'll come with you. When you come back to run the last few tests on Eve. I'll see this through to the end.'

- - -

The sound of screams echoing through the subway station tore me from my sleep. Scrambling out of bed, I ran to the door and threw it open. The corridor beyond was lit by a flickering orange and red light, as though illuminated by dancing flames. Twisted shadows flickered across the edges of my vision. Running toward the source of the cries, I rounded a corner and tripped over a body lying sprawled on the floor.

The wall next to it was decorated with a spray of blood, black in the hellish light that played over the hallway. I knelt down and saw that it was Mercer, sightless eyes staring off into the distance and a ragged hole where his throat used to be. Looking up, I saw a cloaked figure at the far end of the hall. Blue eyes glinted beneath the hood that concealed her features, but I could tell that it was Eve. She turned and fled out of sight, laughter echoing off the walls of the corridor.

Pulling myself to my feet, I ran heedlessly after her and emerged in the wide tunnel at the southern end of the station. A dozen more bodies, all with faces I recognised, lay scattered across the floor in wide pools of black blood. Eve stood at the platform ahead, her back toward me, and I moved with deadly purpose towards her. A flash of movement to my left caught my eye and I turned to see Eve step out from the shadows. Another movement to my right and a third Eve exited a service corridor on the other side of the tunnel.

106

Another two Eves joined the two in the tunnel with me, boxing me in. The air was thick and hot, burning my lungs as though I'd stuck my head into a furnace. I felt something in my hand and looked down to find the handle of a scalpel clutched tightly in my fist, its blade long and wicked sharp.

Snarling in frustration, I spun on my heel and bolted toward the one standing on top of the platform. I flew up the makeshift steps to confront her and saw that she held Davin by his throat. He struggled weakly, looking toward me with desperate eyes. I had barely taken a step toward them when there was a resounding crack. The sound echoed across the platform as Davin slumped lifeless to the ground.

I screamed wordlessly, slashing the scalpel toward her as she turned to face me. The blade sliced across her throat before I realised that it was Madeleine, not Eve, that stood before me. Her eyes narrowed in accusation as a thick curtain of dark crimson swept down from the wound and her mouth opened as if to say something. Blood bubbled out from between her lips and she collapsed to the ground, dead. I dropped the scalpel, horrified at what I'd done, and scrambled over to check on Davin.

Except it wasn't Davin. It looked like him, but his features were too angular, his skin grey and pallid. His eyes flicked open, a blazingly bright blue, and he smiled at me with a mouth full of needle-like teeth. I recoiled from him and suddenly I was surrounded. A circle of monsters crowded around me, their laughter mocking and cruel. Some were Eve, some were not-Davin, some were other faces I did not recognise, but all were clearly recognisable as my creations.

Grey, corpse-like hands reached out toward me, grabbing me and pinning me down. I started to scream, fighting against the inexorable tide of bodies that crushed down on me.

A jarring pain flared through my shoulder as I landed on the floor of my bedroom, limbs tangled with my bedsheets. I lay still in the darkness, drenched in sweat, my breath coming in short, shallow gasps.

The dream weighed heavily on my mind as I went about my usual business that night. Nightmares were a regular occurrence for me—their dark shadows had plagued me for years. They were seldom meaningless, often relating to my experiments, to Eve, or to Travis' death. It was then that I realised that perhaps there was more to them than guilt and fear. Perhaps my subconscious was trying to warn me?

Once the hydroponics were taken care of and the few minor injuries that had occurred that day had been treated, I sat by myself in my room, staring morosely at the wall.

Eve was strong, physically as well as mentally. She was preternaturally tough, better adapted to survive in the harsh conditions of the outside world and resistant to the radiation that was slowly killing humanity. *Homo sapiens superior.* She wanted a companion, someone to share her life with so that she did not have to be alone. What consequences would come of that?

If she carried the child to term and gave birth to him, it would prove that I had indeed solved the issue of infertility, but what then? She would raise the child to be her companion. The thought made me shudder. He would a genetic clone of Davin, not related to her by blood, but she would still be his 'mother', just as I was hers. Eve would raise him and groom him to be her mate.

He should enjoy all the benefits of his enhanced genetics, just as Eve did, and he would be a monster, just as she was. A fertile monster. Would they breed true? It seemed likely. And with their accelerated growth and maturation, they would breed quickly. A family of monsters.

Two was not enough for a stable breeding population, though. They would die out through inbreeding after a couple of generations. Or would they? Eve had surprised me countless times with new traits inherited from the aggressively dominant plant genes I had modified her DNA with. Could they breed with ordinary people?

Resentment against ordinary humans could build dangerously in a group like that. They might turn raider, kidnapping healthy humans and forcibly breeding with them to swell their numbers. How likely was that to happen? Would that be my legacy? My gift to humanity? An army of monsters, sweeping across the planet, raping, killing, wiping us out once and for all. The original intent behind my experiments, creating new hope for humankind, seemed so far away. Images of grey-skinned monsters, borne of my hubris and unspeakable acts, haunted my every waking thought.

The night we were due to return to the lab to administer the last few tests, I made up my mind. It had gone far enough, this madness of mine, this horror I had created. Eve may not have been at fault, but I simply could not follow through with the promise I had made to her.

That evening, while in the doctors' surgery packing the supplies I would need to perform the pregnancy tests, I retrieved an additional small plastic container from the locked medicine cabinet. Trepidation filled me as I popped open the lid to inspect the contents. Two small pill bottles, labelled mifepristone and misoprostol. Chemical abortifacients. They had been found at one of the hospital pharmacies long ago, but I had never expected to ever have to use them. A pregnancy is something to be celebrated and treasured—children rare and precious. My intentions seemed monstrous even to me, but I steeled myself and continued on. After stowing them away in my pack I had to reread one of my medical textbooks to double-check that they were all I needed to perform the abortion. I met Madeleine at the southern exit and we left for the laboratory.

'It worked,' I said. 'You're pregnant.' I threw away the testing agent I had used to confirm the pregnancy.

She smiled, closing her eyes and placing a hand on her stomach. 'Thank you.'

My mouth went dry and I turned to my backpack, rummaging about for a few moments before taking out the plastic container. I took a moment to steady myself—my breathing had sped up and I could feel my heart thudding in my chest. Popping the lid open, I took out the bottle of misoprostol before shakily setting it down on the table beside me. Unscrewing the lid, I upended it and carefully shook one of the white tablets into the palm of my hand. After a moment's consideration, I tapped the bottle on my fingers to dislodge a second then turned to Eve.

'Here.' I held out my hand. Eve reached out and took the pills from me. I picked up a plastic bottle of water and offered it to her as well. She didn't question it at all, just placing the tablets at the back of her tongue and washing them down her throat with a swallow of water. I put the misoprostol back into the plastic container and took out the bottle of mifepristone. 'There are two tablets in here. You'll need to take them the day after tomorrow, okay?'

110

'All right.' Eve nodded and took the bottle from me, looking at the half-torn label. 'Mifepristone,' she read aloud.

Madeleine looked at me, head tilting to one side as her brow furrowed questioningly. I had not told her about my plan to dose Eve with the abortifacients, of course, but she should not have recognised the name of the compound, either. 'It should regulate your hormones,' I stammered slightly, caught off balance by the way Madeleine had looked at me. 'Make sure that everything goes smoothly.'

'Okay.'

'We should go.' I glanced longingly in the direction of the door. 'This is it. We won't see you again.'

Eve sighed softly. 'Okay. Goodbye, Del. Maddy. I'm sorry I ruined everything. I'm sorry about Travis. Thank you for doing this for me. Take care of yourselves.'

'You too,' I said. I tried to smile, but my mouth twisted itself into a humourless grimace. My hands were clammy with sweat and I fidgeted as I stood there, my nerves raw. Looking over at Madeleine, I gestured towards the door with a tilt of my head.

'Goodbye, Eve,' she said, retrieving her flashlight from the table she had rested it on and starting toward the exit.

I waited until she had walked past to pick up my backpack and sling it over my shoulder. Nodding at Eve for what I hoped was the last time, I followed Madeleine's lead, crossing the tiled floor to exit. We slipped through the gap between the doors and were halfway between there and the elevator when I heart a quiet gasp of pain and surprise behind me. I froze, my senses suddenly on alert.

'Del?' Eve called. 'Wait, my stomach hurts. I think something's wrong.'

111

I took a shaky step forward, toward the elevator. That was impossible. According to what I'd read, the medication took a couple of days to work and even then it wasn't enough to abort a foetus on its own. It was supposed to merely halt the pregnancy, damaging the uterine lining to the point that when the misoprostol was taken it would easily flush out uterus and abort the foetus.

The bottom dropped out of my stomach as it dawned on me. I felt like throwing up. Misoprostol was the one that flushed the uterus. Mifepristone was the one that started the process. Somehow, I had managed to mix up the names of the compounds. I'd administered the wrong drug. Eve gave a small yelp of pain, calling my name again.

Madeleine took a hesitating step back toward the laboratory but I didn't move. 'We should go back for her,' she said.

Licking my lips, I tried to think of an excuse, any excuse, that would justify us abandoning her to her fate. Nothing came to mind and I simply nodded dumbly instead. Together, we hurried back down the hallway to the lab doors. Eve stood just inside, hunched over in pain, one hand across her stomach as though she were stopping her insides from falling out.

'We're here,' Madeleine said as she went to Eve's side to help support her weight. 'Let's get you to a bed so you can lie down.' She started to move her toward the back of the lab, step by shaky step.

We moved her to the bottom bunk in what had been my bedroom when I had taken to living in the lab all those years ago. She curled up on the bed, grimacing in pain. My mind raced as I tried to decide what to do. Even with the mix-up, the abortifacient should not have taken effect so quickly. It should have been at least an hour before Eve started getting cramps. 'You must be having some sort of reaction to the compound,' I thought aloud.

'What can we do?'

'Nothing,' I blurted out. 'We have to let it run its course. We can treat her symptoms, though. Give her something for the pain.' Unshouldering my pack as Eve groaned in pain, clutching at her stomach, I made a show of rummaging about looking for pain killers.

'Adele…' Madeleine's voice held a note of urgency.

Looking up, I saw her standing toward the foot of the bed, her flashlight illuminating Eve's bottom half. A dark stain had started spreading across the sheets, black and ugly in the harsh light. I pulled away and Eve looked up at me, desperate eyes full of tears. 'Del, it hurts,' she whimpered. 'Do something. Please.'

There was nothing I could do. I fled the room, seeking reprieve in the dark corridor outside. Behind me Eve's alarmed voice called my name again but I ignored it, resting my forehead against the cool wall and squeezing my eyes shut. This wasn't how it was supposed to have happened. Eve should have been on her own, far from here, when her pregnancy terminated itself. I wasn't supposed to be here to witness what I had done to her.

What sort of a person did that make me? Confronted by the results of my handiwork this day, I was having trouble deciding who was the monster—was it Eve; the young girl, crying and scared and in pain? Or was it me?

After a time there was a quiet shuffle of movement, the black behind my eyelids rudely interrupted by light shining on me. I lifted my head, holding out a hand to shield my eyes as I opened them. Madeleine looked back at me from the doorway, her expression hard. She lowered her flashlight as she walked over toward me, her eyes searching my face. I met her gaze, sure that she would see the shame and guilt written plainly across my features. Minutes passed as we stood across from each other in silence.

A dark shape appeared in the doorway behind her. Eve. Stumbling slightly, she took a step forward. 'It was you, wasn't it?' she asked. 'You did this...on purpose?'

I opened my mouth to try to say something, but no words came. Instead I looked away, my face burning.

'Why?' Eve's voice quavered, grief mixed with confusion. 'I don't understand. Why? Del, why?'

'I'm sorry.'

'You promised!' Anger started to seep into her tone. 'You promised me I wouldn't be alone! How could you?' Her breathing was coming fast and erratic. Madeleine turned and reached out to steady her with a hand on her shoulder, but Eve recoiled from her touch. 'I hate you!' she screamed. 'I hate you! I hate you! I hate you!'

There was a blur of movement in the corner of my eye and Madeleine gave a startled cry as her flashlight smashed against the wall of the corridor, the LEDs winking out and plunging us into darkness. Adrenaline surged into my system and I pulled away from the wall, eyes wide and unseeing in the sudden blackness. I had left my own flashlight in the bedroom, and I fumbled at my side for the gun holstered there.

Something slammed into my chest, knocking the wind from me, and I fell to the ground. My head hit the tiled floor with a crack and my thoughts fled from me, disappearing into a foggy cloud of pain. My arms and legs refused to obey, flailing about weakly as I tried to struggle into a sitting position. My head felt as though it had floated off my shoulders, rendering me a detached observer trying to control a body that wasn't mine. I was vaguely aware of hands on me, a dragging sound somewhere off past my feet, and then the darkness claimed me.

- - -

My head throbbed, my mind swimming groggily back into consciousness. I shifted slightly and a lance of agony stabbed through the back of my neck, tingling all the way to the tips of my fingers. Yellow and purple spots danced in front of my eyes, starkly contrasted against the pitch black. I simply lay still, gasping in pain like a fish deprived of water as I tried not to move.

Gathering my strength, I eventually worked up enough to pull myself up against the wall. The cool solidity of it beneath my back gave me something to focus on outside of the pain. I fought to stand. My head spun, threatening to send me crashing back to the floor, but I held on to the wall, grimly refusing to give up.

Dimly, I noted that it was likely I was suffering from a severe concussion. Cautiously reaching up to feel the back of my head, I sucked air in through my teeth and winced as a fresh wave of pain flooded over me. Dried blood greeted my questing fingertips, but it didn't feel as though I had cracked my skull open. Focusing on my breathing, I willed myself to follow the wall in what I hoped was the direction of the bedroom.

An age seemed to pass as I took one shuffling step after another. Eventually I reached the doorframe. Entering the room, I tried to remember exactly where I had left my flashlight, hoping that it would still be there. An attempt to cross the room to the spot where I thought my backpack lay sent me crashing to my knees, tears stinging my eyes as I crawled the rest of the way. My pack and flashlight were where I had left them, near the head of the bunk beds.

When the light flicked on I let out an involuntary yelp of pain, the sudden illumination scouring my eyes like acid. I hugged the flashlight to my chest, pointed downwards to muffle the brightness. Concentrating on my breathing, I reached into my pack and fumbled with the medical kit inside, spilling its contents across the floor. Opening one eye just a crack so I could see, I reached out and groped at the various bottles until I found what I thought was the one I was looking for. Vicodin.

The flashlight dropped from my hands, temporarily forgotten, as I unscrewed the cap with both hands. I tried to dump the contents into my shaking hand, but the dozen pills left in the bottle fell to the ground and scattered. Picking two off the ground, I swallowed them greedily, forcing them down my dry throat.

After a while, a pleasant sort of numb warmth spread through my body, starting in the centre of my chest and moving outward. The pain dulled, dropping to a more bearable level. I pulled myself back to my feet. My limbs moved sluggishly, but the movements were at least no longer accompanied by spikes of pain.

My fuzzy thoughts turned to Madeleine. Taking up my flashlight, I stumbled back out of the room, squinting as my eyes tried and failed to adjust to the singular beam of light cutting through the blackness. There was no sign of Maddy or Eve. The only evidence that marred the corridor was a small patch of half-dry blood, likely where my head had hit the floor, and the smashed remains of Maddy's flashlight. My hand went to the holster at my side, but the gun was missing.

Returning to the bedroom, I made a half-hearted effort to gather the contents of my medical kit and stuff them back into my pack. Once I had, I slipped my arms into the straps and secured it to my back. The beam of my flashlight lingered on the bed beside me for a moment, illuminating the wide patch of dark crimson that stained it.

My thoughts turned to escape. I briefly considered calling out for Madeleine, but fear of Eve returning for me kept me quiet. There was little I could do for my friend in my current state in any case, and I had been unconscious for who knew how long. If Eve wanted to hurt Maddy, it was too late for me to help her. Silently, I prayed for her safety. Madeleine had been like a mother to Eve. I hoped that that was enough to save her life.

Steeling myself, I slowly started down the corridor, heading toward the main workroom. Nothing hindered my passage, though I started a few times at what I thought was movement in the corner of my eye. The main laboratory was similarly devoid of obstacles. I made my way out the main doors, heading toward the elevator.

Climbing up through the roof of the elevator into the shaft was a significant effort, my arms protesting heavily as I forced them to lift my weight. A bout of dizziness claimed me as I stumbled onto the top of the elevator, forcing me to sit down and spend a few moments steadying myself before continuing.

One set of the ropes that Madeleine and I had used on our way down to the lab was missing. Someone had already ascended ahead of me. I tried to tell myself that it was probably Madeleine, gone to get help, though I knew that the chances of that were almost nil. Standing, I clipped myself to the climbing rope.

The ascent to the top of the elevator shaft was hard, harder than anything else I've ever done. It felt like it took hours, my muscles screaming at me as I slowly pulled myself upwards. Twice, my arms gave out and I fell back to the bottom of the shaft, barely managing to catch the rope and stop myself from meeting the same fate as my brother. Each time, I managed to find it within myself to get back up and start over. I began to despair that I would never reach the top, my concussed and pain-addled mind imagining that I was trapped in a hellish punishment like that of Sisyphus, condemned to repeat the climb again and again for all eternity.

Somehow, my efforts eventually paid off. I found myself at the top, scrabbling at the bottom of the elevator doors, grabbing hold and heaving myself onto the floor of the ground level. I stopped to catch my breath for a while, mopping up the sweat pouring from my brow with the bottom of my shirt. Retrieving a bottle of water from my pack, I drank from it with cracked lips. Once I was ready, I began the walk back to Sécheron.

My head was pounding when I made it to the final stretch of tunnels leading into the subway station. Each beat of my heart thudded heavily in my ears, driving a new spike of fresh agony into my brain. There were some people around, though I had trouble focusing on their faces. I approached them, asking to be taken to Mercer. Someone took hold of my arm to steady me, asking if I was okay. I mumbled something in response and several voices started talking at once, my ears unable to separate out the individual words.

Strong hands guided me into the station. I blinked, finding myself being laid down in one of the beds in the doctor's surgery. I tried to sit back up, still mumbling that I needed to see Mercer right away, but someone gently and firmly pushed me back into bed. I was given water and eventually my head cleared enough that I saw Davin peered down at me, his expression worried.

My eyes focused on him. 'I need to see Mercer,' I insisted.

'Shhh, Adele.' Davin put his hand on my forehead as he shushed me. 'It's okay. It looks like you hit your head pretty hard, but you'll be fine. Just rest.'

'Can't. Need to see Mercer. Madeleine's gone.'

'Gone?' Mercer's voice came from behind Davin, who turned to look at him. The older man came to the head of the bed and knelt down beside me, his eyes narrowed. He took my hand and squeezed it softly. 'Adele, what do you mean she's gone?'

'Eve took her.'

There was a moment of silence and the two men exchanged worried glances. 'No one has seen Eve since Travis died,' Davin said. 'Are you sure, Adele?'

'She attacked us. Hit my head. When I woke up they were both gone.'

'You stay here with her. I'll arrange a search party.' Mercer stood, addressing Davin before looking back down at me. 'Where, Adele? Where were you attacked?'

'Lab.'

Mercer frowned for a moment, looking as though he was about to reprimand me for going back to that place. Instead, he shook his head and turned away, walking out of the room. Davin stood, walking over to the basin to soak a cloth in water. He brought it over, folding it in half before draping it over my forehead.

The cool cloth felt good on my skin. I waved a hand over to where my backpack lay discarded on the ground. I didn't even remember anyone taking it off me. 'Pain meds. Vicodin.'

Following my vague instructions, Davin retrieved the pills from my pack. I took another two, washing them down with a mouthful of water from my half-empty bottle. It was not terribly wise to do so only a scarce handful of hours after having taken my last dose, but I didn't care at that point. It didn't take long for the medication to start to take effect, drowning out the pain with a pleasantly familiar numbness that left my fingers tingling.

Davin remained at my bedside until I felt well enough to stand again, which I did despite his protests. 'There's nothing more you can do,' he said, holding me by the shoulders. 'Mercer and Simon are out looking for Madeleine and Eve. You need to lie down.'

'Need to take care of my head,' I said, taking a deep breath to steady myself. 'Give me a hand.'

Davin did most of the work, cleaning, sterilizing and bandaging my injured head at my direction. It stung, but at the end of the process I was starting to feel a lot better. The concussion would take time to heal, so my head would ache for a good while yet. Apart from that I just needed some time to rest and recover.

I didn't want to stay in the surgery, insisting on returning to my own bed. Davin guided me, holding me gently, as though certain I would fall over and break at any moment. I let him, grateful for the feel of his body close to mine. We approached the door to my room but stopped at the threshold.

The lamp on the table was on. Someone was already in my bed, completely covered by the sheets, lying curled up and facing away from the door. Davin looked at me, his brow furrowed, and gently extricated himself from my grasp. He walked over to the bed, leaving me holding onto the door frame. 'Hey,' he said gently, reaching down to pull back the sheet. There was a beat of silence before he inhaled sharply in shock, taking an involuntary step backward.

I stumbled forward past him to be greeted by the sight of Madeleine lying still on the bed, her dead eyes staring glassily at the wall. Grabbing hold of her shoulders, I shook her violently, screaming her name, as though I could wake her if I tried hard enough. Her head lolled to the side and I broke down in tears, sobs wracking my body as I curled up beside her, the pain in my head forgotten. Davin knelt down, putting his arms around me in a tight embrace and making quiet shushing noises.

That was when the power went out. The lamp beside the bed, the fluorescent bulbs that lit the corridor outside the room—all of them went out, plunging us into darkness. Davin's grip on me loosened slightly as I felt him lift his head alertly. I took a deep breath, swallowing my tears. 'She's here,' I whispered, my voice hoarse. 'Eve is in the station.'

- - -

Davin flicked on the flashlight he had retrieved from its place in the emergency kit under my bed. A single beam of light cut through the darkness, illuminating a patch of the wall. It wasn't much, but it was enough to make me feel a little better about our situation. For once, I was glad that Mercer had always been so insistent on the safety policies that mandated the kits to every occupied room in Sécheron.

'She must have disconnected the battery array. We'll get you somewhere safe and then I'll go and try to bring the power back on.'

'You can't leave me alone,' I said, shaking my head vehemently. 'She deliberately left Madeleine here so I would find her. She'll come for me next.'

'With the lights out everyone else is in danger too, Adele. We need to warn them.'

'If we cause a panic, people will get hurt. Eve might have a grudge against everyone here because of how she was treated growing up, but it's me she wants. I'm the one who made her the way she is and rejected her for it.' I squeezed Davin's arm, reassuring myself that he was there.

'All right.' Davin sounded dubious. 'But we still need to get the lights back on. Gage and Simon would have gone with the others to search for Madeleine. If Eve's damaged the batteries, I don't think there's anyone else left at the station that could fix them but me.'

'And what if Eve attacks us?'

'Where's your gun?'

'I lost it when I hit my head.' I bit my lip, hand nervously touching the empty holster at my side. 'Eve might have it.'

'Great.' Davin took a deep breath, thinking for a moment. 'Okay. Mercer keeps a rifle in his room. It's not far from here,' he said.

'Okay. Let's go, then.'

Davin took the lead as we left my bedroom, sweeping the flashlight from left to right as we moved slowly down the corridor. Were I following him any closer, I'd have stepped on the back of his heels. Straining my ears, I listened for any sign of movement. This was less than helpful. The amount of people in Sécheron guaranteed that there were plenty of sounds to startle me, even more now as people blundered about in the lightless corridors and called out to each other. Echoes in the darkness made my paranoid mind prone to imagining sounds closer than they were. By the time we reached Mercer's room it felt as though I would die of heart failure long before Eve got to me.

Once inside, I closed the door behind us and stood by it while Davin checked over the room to make sure we were alone. Satisfied, he went to the gun cabinet and examined the padlock securing it. 'Ah,' he said. 'It's locked.'

'Can you get it open?'

'I don't think so. It looks pretty sturdy,' Davin swore under his breath. 'If I had the big pair of bolt cutters from the workshop I could get it open.' He shone the flashlight around the room, looking for anything that might help with opening the cabinet.

Knowing Mercer, he probably kept the key on him all the time, but there was still a chance that it was hidden in a desk drawer or something. At the very least, there would be another flashlight in the emergency kit beneath the bed. I touched the handle of the door again to make sure it was shut properly then carefully picked my way across the room to the bed. The kit was underneath, as I knew it would be, but my hands brushed against a second, heavier parcel as well.

I smiled when I undid the cord binding the canvas shut. 'I think this might help,' I said, waving a crowbar in

Davin's general direction. Mercer kept a set of tools under his bed alongside the standard emergency kit.

He took the crowbar off me and wedged the tip of it into the small gap in the cabinet door. The metal bent fairly easily beneath his powerful muscles, squealing slightly in protest. 'Sorry, Mercer,' Davin said, apologising to the empty air. Reaching into the cabinet, he pulled out a hunting rifle and a box of ammunition.

Our next destination was the solar batteries at the highest sheltered level of the subway station. Davin moved quicker this time, flashlight in one hand, crowbar in the other and the loaded rifle slung over one broad shoulder. Now that we were armed and I was able to keep a proper eye on our rear, I began to feel a little bit safer.

Ahead of us, the corridor opened out into the nearer of the two hydroponics platforms and we could see the glow from another pair of flashlights bobbing around past the entrance. 'Hey!' Davin called out, 'Is everyone okay?'

'We're fine!' It was Lara's voice. 'Is anyone with you?'

'I'm here, too.' My voice sounded loud in my ears. We emerged into the bottom level of the hydroponics farm, trying not to blind the others with our flashlights. I could see four adult-sized shapes and one child, which I assumed was Jeanette. It was difficult to pick out faces in the indirect light.

'What happened?' someone asked. 'What's wrong with the lights?'

'I don't know,' Davin shook his head 'We're on our way to the solar batteries to see if there's a problem on that end.'

'Do you need any help?'

'It'd be better if we stuck together, less chance of someone hurting themselves in the dark.' Lifting his flashlight, Davin panned the beam over the hydroponics above us. The light sent shadows dancing madly across the far wall and I shivered, imagining how easy it would be for someone to hide up there.

There was a murmur of assent. As a group, we started to move toward the stairs leading up to the platform proper. Davin remained in the lead and I tried to stay behind him, keeping as many bodies between me and my surroundings as possible. Cowardly, I suppose, but I've never professed to being overly courageous.

We reached the platform without incident, making our way past the crops and then up the escalator leading to the level above. Eventually, we reached the battery array. Davin handed me the crowbar and the rifle from his shoulder, focusing on inspecting the connections between the batteries and the lighting system. Lara looked at me curiously but I ignored her, taking up a position near to where Davin stood. I swept my flashlight fearfully over the surrounding area.

A gunshot split the air, almost unbelievably loud. Sparks flew from the metal panel near Davin's head as a bullet ricocheted off it. There were cries of alarm as people ducked, confused and panicky. Dropping the crowbar and flashlight, I brought the rifle up, pulling back the lever and aiming into the darkness as I stepped away from the light.

The wide, curved shape of the concourse we were standing in made it next to impossible to tell where the shot had come from. I hadn't seen a muzzle flash, though, which ruled out the direction I had been looking in. Fingering the trigger, I tried to calm my breathing and keep the rifle steady in my hands.

'Calm, everyone! Keep quiet and stay down!' Davin turned to crowd control, attempting to get everyone to drop to the ground and turn their lights off. He hustled over to me, keeping his head down. 'I think that might have just been a warning shot. We're too exposed here. We need to find cover.'

'That's what she wants. We need to get the lights back on,' I said stubbornly.

'Unless you can convince her not to shoot me while I work, I don't think that's going to happen.'

I made a frustrated noise in the back of my throat. Davin was right. With the lights out and half of the station away looking for Madeleine, this was Eve's game. Briefly, I wondered why she hadn't tried to kill me yet. She only had limited bullets, maybe she hadn't had a clear shot.

Lowering the rifle, I crouched down near to Davin's ear and whispered as quietly as I could, 'She won't risk losing track of me. If I lead everyone away from here, she'll follow. Turn off your light and hide. Once we're gone, you can fix the lights.'

'I don't like this plan,' he hissed back.

'Have you got a better one?'

Davin stared at me for a few moments before shaking his head. 'Okay,' he said. Leaning in suddenly, he kissed me hard on the lips. 'I love you.'

'I love you, too.' I nodded at him and he disappeared into the darkness, heading in the direction of the power cables. 'All right.' I raised my voice slightly so everyone else could hear. 'We need to get to cover. Keep your lights off and take the hand of the person in front of you. Stay low.'

'Who's out there? Who's shooting at us?' Lara demanded, grabbing my wrist as I went to turn away.

'It's Eve,' I said quietly.

She didn't respond. Carefully, I put down the rifle and reached out to grab my flashlight from where it had fallen. Once I had it, I turned it off and tucked it awkwardly into my pants. Picking the weapon back up in one hand, I tugged at Lara's arm with the other and started to slowly lead the group toward the far side of the concourse. There was a second escalator there that would take us down to the other hydroponics platform and from there we'd hopefully be able to make it back to the service corridors. The tighter quarters would make it much harder for Eve to sneak up on us.

We were halfway across when the sound of several pairs of feet running up the escalator behind us made me pause. Looking back, I saw bobbing lights appear as three people with torches entered the concourse from the same direction as we had.

'Hello?' one of them shouted. 'We heard a shot! Is anyone hu—'

He was cut off with an 'oof' sound, as though he had been winded. The first flashlight went flying off into the darkness, going out with a clatter as it smashed against a wall. There was another shout, some thuds followed by yelps of pain and surprise. The other two lights went out as well. The silence that followed hung thick and heavy and I hesitated, unsure of what to do.

'We have to go back,' Lara hissed at me. 'They need help.'

Tightening my grip on the stock of the rifle, I nodded to myself. 'You go back and take care of them,' I said. 'I'll distract her. She wants me.'

'I don't know what's going on, Adele, but you and your crazy bitch daughter can both go straight to hell.' Lara threw off my hand and scuttled away into the darkness. I waited for the shuffling footsteps to retreat a fair distance away, taking out my flashlight again and cranking the handle a few times.

Once I had judged that they had moved far enough away, I rose to my feet and flicked on the light, waving it madly across the concourse to attract attention to myself. 'Eve! Come and get me!' I yelled, then turned and ran.

It took a handful of seconds for me to cross the open ground to the second escalator. My breath came in short, sharp gasps as my heart pounded in my chest. I managed to make it to the top of the escalator in one piece. No shots had rung out, no bullets slammed into me. Without stopping to catch my breath, I flew down the stairs two at a time, moving as quickly as I could without tripping over my own flailing feet.

I slowed once I reached the bottom, more because I was already out of breath than by choice. Ducking down between the rows of hydroponic troughs, I flicked off my flashlight to hide in the darkness and tried to listen for the sound of pursuit. Unfortunately, my own ragged breathing and my pulse thudding in my ears were more than enough to drown out most other noises.

Hoping that Eve wasn't sure exactly where I was, I raised my head above the trough I was hiding behind. With one hand, I threw my flashlight as hard as I could, sending it flying off into the gloom in a high arc. It landed with a clatter somewhere at the far side of the room. I strained my eyes to look for any sign of movement that might give away Eve's position.

After a few minutes had crawled past, there was a sudden yell from the concourse above. Davin's voice. I stood bolt upright, levelling my rifle at the top of the escalator.

Licking my lips, I started to slowly walk forward. An oddly-shaped silhouette appeared at the railing overlooking the hydroponics. I aimed my weapon at it, hesitating.

The dark shape seemed to struggle with itself for a moment, then part of it broke off and plummeted over the edge of the concourse. There was a sickening crack as the shape jerked to a sudden stop and hung there, halfway between the railing and the hydroponics below. My eyes fixed on the dangling shape. It was a body, of that I was sure, but I couldn't make out exactly how big it was or who it might be.

I saw movement out of the corner of my eye and I swung my rifle around to aim at a dark shape bounding down the escalator steps. 'Davin!' I called out, but it did not slow down or respond. Raw panic rising in my chest, I squeezed the trigger. The rifle jumped in my hands, slamming its butt back into my shoulder.

Wincing in pain, I groped at the lever to pull it back for a second shot. Across from me, amongst the hydroponics troughs, a flashlight flicked on. Eve held it so that the beam shined up and illuminated her face, glinting green off her eyes. She was looking directly at me. As I swung the rifle around to aim at her, she moved the flashlight, looking over and using it to point back toward the concourse.

Davin's body hung from the railing, slowly spinning. An orange climbing rope was tied in a noose around his neck. The hunting rifle dropped, forgotten, from my nerveless fingers. I stood there in shock. I couldn't move. Couldn't speak. Couldn't think.

'Now you know what it's like,' Eve's voice whispered in my ear. 'You're all alone now. Just like me.'

Then she left.

I sank slowly to the ground, squeezing my eyes shut. Willing her to come back and finish me off. Inside, it felt like my organs were being torn up, my stomach clenched so tight that I could scarcely breathe. My face burned with heat, my eyes stinging with tears as a great weight pressed down on my shoulders, suffocating me. Davin had been all that I'd had left. Now he was gone. Maddy was gone. Travis was gone. I was all alone.

- - -

'Are you sure this is what you want?'

Mercer lingered in the doorway, unsure whether his entry would be an intrusion or not. Food rations were piled high at one end of my bed, next to a couple of sets of spare clothes and a basic kit of medical supplies. A rifle leant against the mattress, next to a box of ammunition and my pistol. Everything was slowly being packed away as I ticked off my mental checklist.

I glanced toward the door. 'I'm sure.'

'We'll struggle here without a proper doctor. It was hard enough when Travis died, but with you gone too...' Mercer walked slowly into the room as he spoke, stopping once he stood beside me. 'We'll manage. After everything that's happened, this is probably for the best.'

'Sécheron has survived worse,' I said, turning to look at him properly for a moment. If I could have, I would have smiled. 'You're a good leader. I'm sorry I never listened to you.'

He barked out a short, mirthless laugh. 'So am I, but then I never really expected you to. You're too much like your mother. I promised her I'd look after you, you know? Before she died.'

'You did what you could.'

We stood in silence for a few minutes as I finished stowing away my supplies. Experimentally, I took hold of one of the backpack's shoulder straps and hefted it, testing the weight. Satisfied, I started to double-check my rifle and pistol, taking them apart and methodically cleaning each part.

Mercer watched me quietly as I worked. 'Are you sure she'll have left?' he said once I had reassembled the guns.

I nodded, securing the pistol in the holster at my side. 'There's nothing more for her here, unless she wants to watch me suffer. She'll try to move on, get away from all the memories here.' Even if I was wrong and Eve did want to torment me more, remaining in Sécheron would only put the community at risk. It was better for everyone if I left.

'How will you find her?'

'I don't know yet, but I will. Whatever it takes.'

Eve already had a two-day head start on me. With any luck, she wouldn't suspect that I intended to pursue her. She would have to stop at other settlements for food and medicine and she wasn't at all familiar with the world outside Geneva. Les Charmilles then, would be a likely place to start looking, or perhaps Chêne-Bourg. Tracking her down would be difficult, but determination burned in my chest like a bonfire. Someone, somewhere would see her and I would pick up her trail. Picking up the backpack, I slid my arms through the shoulder straps and adjusted them so it sat reasonably comfortably.

'It won't bring them back,' Mercer said, his voice soft.

'I know.' I took a deep breath, blinking away tears, and turned to look at him again. 'There needs to be an end to this. For my sake and for hers.'

He stared at me a moment, then nodded. 'Goodbye, Adele. I hope you find some measure of peace.'

Picking up the rifle, I shook my head sadly and turned toward the door. 'There will never be any peace for me. Goodbye, Mercer.'

- - -

Adele fell back into unconsciousness, murmuring nonsense words under her breath.

The room's other occupant remained silently by her bedside for a time. It wouldn't be long now, perhaps another day or so, before she passed on. The room smelt faintly of charred meat. The lingering scent had turned his stomach when he had found Adele, sun scorched and half dead, less than two hundred metres from the entrance to the London Underground at Shoreditch. There had been little he could do but ease her suffering—he hadn't the heart to leave her out to die or even to put her out of her misery.

When she had started rambling in French, it had caught his attention. There were very few native French speakers in London—his own mother had been from Paris and so he had learned the language from a young age. When Adele had told him that she was from Geneva and began recounting her strange story, his curiosity was piqued. Very few traders dared to brave the barren waste of the English Channel, so news from what remained of continental Europe was rare. From then, he had remained by her side right up until the conclusion of her tale.

There had been several occasions when he had been sure that she was too weak to continue. However, even as her blackened lips cracked and bled something pushed her onwards, a fierce determination to finish telling her tale before she died. Though there was a sincerity to her voice and character that rang true, he was not altogether sure how much of her story he believed. At least, until he returned to the room the following morning to check on her.

When he opened the door he saw a figure, clad in a rough cloak of sackcloth, kneeling by the bedside. Rising sharply as he entered, the stranger turned to face him. Beneath the cloak's hood, red-rimmed eyes reflected the light from the lantern he held, glinting green in the gloom. Even in the weak light, he could see her grey skin, her sharp features. Adele's face had been burned by the sun before he had found her, but he imagined that before then she had looked somewhat like the woman now standing in front of him.

'Eve?' he ventured.

'I'm crying,' her voice was ragged, grief-stricken. 'Why am I crying? After everything she did, everything she put me through, I should be celebrating.'

'She was your mother.'

'She was a *monster*,' Eve spat angrily. 'An arrogant, evil monster who didn't care at all about the consequences of anything she did.' Eve took a deep, shuddering breath, her shoulders sagging. 'She always pushed me away. She never wanted to be close to me. I wanted her to love me more than anything.'

He shook his head, his voice firm. 'You killed everyone that ever loved you. Adele's brother. Her friend Madeleine. They loved you and took care of you.'

133

'I didn't mean to!' She stumbled back, covering her face with her hands as she sat down heavily on the chair by the bedside. 'I never wanted to hurt anyone.'

'Travis' death was an accident. She said that much. What excuse do you have for the others?'

Eve was silent for a few moments, her shoulders trembling. Not taking his eyes from her, he walked to the other side of the room and placed the lantern on the table. 'I wish I could take it all back,' she said. 'I've been running for so long...I just want to go home.'

John glanced at Adele's pistol, still in its holster, sitting on the table next to the lantern. Eve raised her head to look at him as he picked it up, lifting it nonthreateningly by the barrel. He took a step toward her and offered it to her. 'You don't have a home.'

Eve stared at the weapon for a moment, then wiped her eyes with the back of her hand and took the gun from him. She turned it over in her hands, examining the surface, tracing the ridges in the metal with a finger. 'Why give me this?' she asked, her voice hoarse.

'It was hers,' he said, matter-of-factly. 'You're her daughter, so now it's yours.' He hunkered down next to her, catching her eye. 'Here's how I see it. You have two choices. You could try to move on. Live your life, remember the good times you had with the people you loved and try to forget the way it ended. Or you could give up.'

The gun felt heavy in Eve's hands. She looked back down at it. 'What should I do?'

Slowly easing himself back into a standing position, he exhaled through his lips. 'Not my place to say. For all I know, the things that woman told me aren't even close to the truth. Even if it was, I've done things I'm not proud of either and I'm not in any position to judge you.'

Eve nodded and rose to her feet. 'Thank you.'

Moving to the side to let her pass, he watched her leave. She walked down the corridor, toward the steps leading to the surface. She lingered there for just a moment, sparing him a single glance before pulling her hood close around her features and ascending the stairs into the sunlight.

POST-APOCALYPTIC GOTHIC
Prometheus' Daughter

- - -

Matthew Karabache is addicted to stories of all kinds, devouring those made up by others and creating his own with equal gusto. Mythology and folklore hold a special fascination for him and he plunders them for ideas and other riches like some sort of literary pirate. He has been writing for as long as he can remember and will continue to do so for ever and ever. You can't stop him, so there. He lives in Brisbane, Australia with his partner Yolanda and her grumpy Manchester terrier.